BUTTERCREAM BUMP OFF

This Large Print Book carries the
Seal of Approval of N.A.V.H.

BUTTERCREAM
BUMP OFF

JENN MCKINLAY

WHEELER PUBLISHING
A part of Gale, Cengage Learning

GALE
CENGAGE Learning™

Detroit • New York • San Francisco • New Haven, Conn • Waterville, Maine • London

GALE
CENGAGE Learning™

LIBRARY OF CONGRESS CATALOGING-IN-PUBLICATION DATA

McKinlay, Jenn.
    Buttercream bump off / by Jenn McKinlay.
      p. cm. — (Wheeler Publishing large print cozy mystery)
    ISBN-13: 978-1-4104-3782-2 (softcover)
    ISBN-10: 1-4104-3782-5 (softcover)
    1. Bakers—Fiction. 2. Bakeries—Fiction. 3.
Murder—Investigation—Fiction. 4. Large type books. I. Title.
PS3612.A948B87 2011
813'.6—dc22   2011008807

Published in 2011 by arrangement with The Berkley Publishing Group, a member of Penguin Group (USA) Inc.

Printed in the United States of America
1 2 3 4 5 6 7 15 14 13 12 11

For the Hub, Chris Hansen Orf.
To quote your own song back to you:
"I'll still love you when
I'm dust and bone."

ACKNOWLEDGMENTS

For the love of cupcakes! I want to acknowledge all of the wonderful readers who have taken Mel, Angie, and Tate into their hearts. I am just delighted that so many of you "get it"! It's been such a pleasure hearing from you all. Special thanks to Mat Matazzoni for entering and winning the "Name the Cupcake" contest. You're in these pages somewhere — have fun finding you!

As always, a special thanks to the dudes, Beckett and Wyatt. Thanks for your help in the kitchen as we experiment with our cupcake recipes and for making me laugh, especially when we suffer cupcake fail.

Thanks to my families, the McKinlays and the Orfs, for your constant encouragement. It means more than I can ever say.

Props to Jessica Faust, agent extraordinaire; Kate Seaver, the ultimate editor; Katherine Pelz, the gifted assistant editor; Andy Ball, the brilliant copyeditor; and

Megan Swartz, PR whiz. I could never manage any of this without all of you.

And here's a shout-out to all of my pals in the kitchen (my fellow bloggers at the Mystery Lover's Kitchen) and my writer pals, the ladies of the loop. Also, thanks to my dear, dear friends for coming to the signings, buying the books, and for enjoying this e-ticket ride almost as much as I do! Love you all!

ONE

"You need to get to the corner of Fifth Avenue and Scottsdale Road. Now."

"Angie?" Melanie Cooper barely recognized her business partner's voice through her sleep-induced haze. "What's going on?"

"Fifth and Scottsdale," Angie DeLaura repeated. The phone went dead.

Mel glanced at the cell phone in her hand then at her alarm clock, which read 6:57. A phone call this early in the morning had better mean Angie's car had been stolen or was on fire.

She heaved off her comforter and rolled out of bed. Mel didn't like mornings on the best of days, but in January, even in Scottsdale, Arizona, it surely was a crime to be dragged out of bed before the sun, especially without a cup of coffee to chase away the morning chill. Still, Angie had been her best friend for more than twenty years. She wouldn't have called if it wasn't important.

That thought got Mel moving. She grabbed a thick-hooded sweatshirt and tugged it on over her flannel pajamas. She could feel the static raise her short blonde hair up, and she imagined she looked like a troll doll on a bad-hair day, without the cute belly button. She jammed her feet into her slip-on sneakers and grabbed her keys.

Mel lived in a snug studio apartment above their cupcake bakery, Fairy Tale Cupcakes, in the heart of Old Town Scottsdale. Angie was her partner, along with their other childhood friend, Tate Harper, who was their main investor. The corner of Fifth and Scottsdale was only a block away. She could be there in minutes.

She pounded down the back stairs and hurried to her red Mini Cooper, which was parked in an adjacent lot. Two quick rights later, she slid into a parking spot in front of an art gallery. The commuter traffic was just beginning, and the intersection ahead of her had an impressive line of cars waiting for the light to change.

Mel spotted Angie sitting on a wooden bench just south of the corner. She didn't appear to be sporting burns or lacerations, so a car accident was out of the question.

"What's up?" Mel asked as she slid onto the bench beside her.

"Wait for it," Angie said and handed her a large, steaming latte in a tall paper cup.

Mel's will to live increased tenfold.

"Wait for . . . ?"

Angie held up her hand, and Mel took a sip from her cup, knowing it would do no good to press. Angie was stubborn like that.

The steaming swallow of java was halfway down her throat when she glanced up and saw a six-foot-tall cupcake come around the corner. Her coffee shot back up her throat, and she erupted into a fit of coughing, causing Angie to pound her on the back.

Mel shoved her aside as soon as she could drag in a breath and goggled at the enormous pink confection strutting between the idling vehicles. It took only a moment to recognize her archenemy, but there was no doubt about it. The giant cupcake was Olivia Puckett!

She was wearing an electric blue satin skirt, pleated accordion style and topped by a pink puffy blouse, stuffed to resemble a gob of frosting and beaded to give it a sprinkle effect. She wore this over bright blue support hose and broad white high heels. A big, round cherry sat on top of her head, tied under her chin like a bonnet. She was handing out hot pink flyers, one of which Angie shoved into Mel's hands.

Free Cupcakes! it read in bold print. It was a coupon for anyone who entered Confections, Olivia's rival bakery.

"Do you think it's a felony to hit a cupcake with your car?" Mel asked.

"Hard to say. You might want to check with Uncle Stan first," Angie said.

Mel's Uncle Stan was a detective with the Scottsdale Police Department. She supposed she could ask him, but somehow she didn't think she'd like the answer.

The light changed, and they watched as the enormous cupcake was caught in the crosswalk and had to hustle her pleated derriere out of the way before the rude honks escalated to rude hand gestures.

It was then, as she tottered onto the curb trying to catch her balance, that the giant cupcake spotted Angie and Mel. She gave them a calculated glance as if she considered them potential customers, but then recognition kicked in. Her ingratiating smile morphed into a look of haughty disdain — impressive with a cherry the size of a bowling ball on her head — and she turned away from them with her nose in the air.

"You'd think after her shenanigans last year Olivia would strive to maintain a lower profile," Angie said.

"You'd think," Mel agreed. "But what

kind of nemesis would she be if she crawled off and disappeared?"

"True," Angie said. "Where would we channel all of our misdirected rage if we didn't have Ginormica Cupcake?"

A horn blared, and they glanced up to see a silver Lexus pass by Olivia, who dropped her basket of flyers in surprise. The Lexus zoomed past, and Mel recognized the driver as Tate, their business partner. Before she could retrieve her basket, Olivia's pink coupons were scattered by a blast of exhaust from a passing Escalade. The scene looked like an impromptu ticker tape parade.

Mel felt Angie nudge her as a motorcycle cop with his lights flashing pulled up alongside the giant cupcake. Over the roar of traffic it was impossible to hear the conversation, but judging by Olivia's wild hand gestures and bobbing cherry hat, it wasn't going her way.

Just then, Tate pulled up beside them and said, " 'What we're dealing with here is a complete lack of respect for the law.' "

"Buford T. Justice, *Smokey and the Bandit*," Mel said, identifying the line. "That's such a man movie."

"It's a classic," Tate said as he pushed open the passenger door.

Mel glanced up and saw Olivia pointing

in their direction. The police officer was studying them over the top of his sunglasses.

"We can debate what constitutes a classic later," Angie said and gave Mel a shove into the car. "Get in! Put the pedal to the metal, Bandit!"

Tate stepped on the gas, and they shot out into traffic. Mel and Angie smiled and waved as they passed Olivia while the officer scribbled a citation on his pad, tore it off, and handed it to Olivia with a flourish. She looked ready to spit sprinkles at them, and Mel sank back into her seat, clutching her latte with a smile.

"Well, that was worth waking up for," she said.

Tate circled the block and parked in front of Fairy Tale Cupcakes.

He opened the car doors for Angie and Mel and said, "We should probably wait before we go get your cars."

"Good idea," Mel said. "I have to prep for my couples' cooking class tonight anyway."

"Ah, yes, your lead-up to Valentine's Day," he said. "How's that going?"

"Five couples for four weekly nights of baking fun," Mel said. "Other than the Bickersons, it's going well."

"Bickersons?" he asked.

"That's what we call the Bakersons," Angie said. "Neither one of them knows a pastry bag from a garbage bag, but they'll fight to the death about it."

"Some couples are like that," Tate said.

Angie fished the keys to the shop out of her purse and led the way into the bakery.

Mel glanced at Tate out of the corner of her eye as she followed him into the shop. It had been three months since his fiancée had been murdered, and even though he had been duped into getting engaged to her — she had been a wily one — Mel wondered if the upcoming lovers' holiday was making him wistful.

"Thank God I don't have to buy anyone flowers or candy or even a card," he said. He shuddered in his impeccably cut navy blue Armani suit. Well, that answered that.

Angie glanced at him with a small smile. " 'Hearts will never be practical until they can be made unbreakable.' "

The Wizard of Oz," Tate said, identifying the quote. "Nice."

Angie bowed her head in acknowledgment before flicking on the overhead lights.

"For the record, my heart is not broken," he protested. "Merely dented."

Angie grinned at him, and Mel felt an anxiety butterfly flap its wings down in her belly. How could Tate not see that when Angie smiled at him her heart was in her eyes? She literally lit up from the inside. A beautiful girl to begin with, when she looked at Tate she was breathtaking.

Mel was torn between wanting to smack Tate into getting a clue and keeping him ignorant for the sake of their friendship. After all, what if Angie and Tate did get together? She'd be shut out of their coupledom. She wasn't sure she was ready for that.

The three of them had met when they were in junior high school. Mel had been a chubby candy freak with no friends until she'd met Tate, who was the consummate geek with thick glasses, starched shirts, and a love of math. Along came Angie, the new kid, with her hot temper and knuckle-cracking ability, and their threesome was formed.

A mutual love of old movies and junk food sealed their friendship all of those years ago. And even now they still spent almost every weekend together watching old movies and eating Jujubes and Milk Duds. There was an ongoing contest between them to see who could stump the others with movie quotes. Mel couldn't help but worry that if Angie and Tate became a couple, she'd be left out.

Tate pushed back his starched cuff and

checked his slim Omega. "Gotta go. Big meeting with the shareholders. Call me if the giant cupcake causes any more trouble."

"Will do," Mel and Angie answered together.

Tate hugged each of them in turn and then left. The bells on the door handle jangled in his wake.

Mel and Angie exchanged a look, and Angie shook her head. "No, I'm not going to tell him how I feel."

"But . . ."

"Change of subject please," Angie said as she pushed through the swinging door into the kitchen beyond. "Like, when are you and Joe going to start playing cars and garages?"

"Playing what?" Mel followed her. Then it clicked. "Oh, I get it. What makes you think we haven't?"

"Oh, please. If you and Joe had slept together, I'd know," she said.

Mel couldn't argue the point. Well, she could, but it would be futile. Angie had known her forever, and Joe was Angie's older brother, the middle one of her seven older brothers, so she'd known him even longer. There was no hiding from Angie.

Mel had lusted after Joe DeLaura from the first time she clapped eyes on him when she was twelve and he was sixteen. And now, they were actually dating. Sometimes she had to pinch herself to believe it. But then, when she remembered they hadn't progressed much past hand-holding, she began to fret.

"Change of subject please," she said.

Angie gave her a knowing nod. "Fine. What are we baking tonight?"

"Kiss Me Cupcakes."

"It sounds as if we could both use a batch of those. Describe please."

Angie dropped her purse on the steel worktable and headed straight for the coffeepot. Mel talked while Angie started a fresh pot.

"It's a mint chocolate chip cupcake with red-and-white swirled mint icing and a big Hershey's Kiss planted in the middle."

"Wrapper on or off?"

"On," Mel said. "I like the silver foil as a decoration."

"Agreed," Angie said. "Oh, hey, one of our couples' payments for class didn't clear. I left the paperwork on your desk. Do you want me to talk to them?"

Mel considered her partner for a second. She didn't think a shakedown from Angie would do anyone any good, so she said, "No, I'll take care of it. But thanks."

"Okay, then. Do I need to run to Smart and Final for any supplies?" Angie asked.

Mel checked the stock in the large plastic bins they kept along one wall of the kitchen. Flour, check. Sugar, check. Baking powder and soda, check. Then she poked her head into the large walk-in refrigerator. Butter, check. Eggs, check. And last, she looked in the pantry for the specialty items. Peppermint extract, check. Chocolate, in all shapes and sizes, check.

"No, I think we're good," she said. "I'm going to grab a shower. Give me fifteen, and we can get started."

"You got it," Angie said. "You do realize, though, that the overstuffed cupcake has issued a challenge that can't be ignored."

"Don't you worry," Mel said. "It won't be. I promise."

Two

Mel pulled her pink bib apron over her head. *Fairy Tale Cupcakes* was scrawled in glittery script over the top, while the bottom half sported three roomy pockets. Angie wore a matching one. The aprons were as close to a uniform as they ventured.

The mint chocolate chip cupcakes had been baked and cooled, and it was now time for the icing. Mel had mixed two batches of peppermint icing, one white and one red. She and Angie then worked in tandem, icing the tops of the cupcakes to look like round peppermint candies.

Angie went first with the white icing. Using medium pressure on the frosting bag, she started in the center and moved the tip out to the edge of the cupcake, allowing the stripe to get wider as she veered to the right, giving it a small curve. Mel followed her lead, filling in the bare spots with red stripes. Mel had thought this would be a good project for their couples, as they would have to work together.

When they finished the last of the twenty-four cupcakes, Angie went back and plopped a shiny silver Hershey's Kiss in the middle of each one.

"Ta da," she said. "Kiss Me Cupcakes. Hey, if the Bickersons start fighting tonight, we can always rename these Kill Me Cupcakes."

"Funny," Mel said with a smile.

Angie hefted the tray of finished cupcakes onto her shoulder while Mel opened the door to the walk-in cooler for her. She then started to clean out her mixers. She had an industrial Hobart and a smaller pink KitchenAid, both of which she would run back to save if the building ever caught fire. Yes, they were covered by insurance, but they were also her babies.

The rest of the day passed by in a blur of buttercream. Three special orders were picked up, one for a mah-jongg club, one for a Girl Scout Daisy troop, and one for the knitting club that met at the yarn shop down the street. Mat Matazzoni, a favorite customer, stopped by to pick up a dozen Calamity Creams, leaving their display case looking empty, which they didn't mind a bit. Between the regulars and the steady stream of foot traffic from tourists visiting Old Town Scottsdale, Mel and Angie rarely had a chance to sit down, catch their breath, or even take a potty break. It appeared that despite Olivia's attempt to steal their customers, Fairy Tale Cupcakes was doing just fine, thank you very much.

"So, have you thought of how we're going to put a crimp in Olivia's cupcake?" Angie asked as she joined Mel in the kitchen to prep for their class.

"Funny you should ask," Mel said. "I did have an idea."

"Let 'er rip, former marketing genius," Angie said.

She was referring to the years before Mel was a pastry chef. As a freshly minted alum from UCLA, Mel had jumped onto the fast track at a marketing firm in Los Angeles. She was a natural, thinking up new and creative ways to move products, and her clients loved her. Too bad she had loathed all things corporate and lived only for her daily sweets fix at her local bakery, which became the catalyst she needed to ditch the job and pursue opening her own bakery. Still, she had skills.

"All I ask is that you keep an open mind," Mel said. She circled the steel worktable, putting out the mixing bowls that their couples would be using.

"Uh-oh." Angie looked concerned as she placed different-size cups with the ingredients already measured in them next to the bowls.

"What?"

"The last time you asked me to have an open mind, you set me up on a blind date with a guy who smelled like onions," Angie said.

"Barry is nice," Mel said.

"He's our accountant," Angie argued. "He's logic and numbers and eau de stinky."

"I was just trying to help," Mel said. "Besides, you set me up with the wandering eyeball."

"Clint is a good guy," Angie protested. "He just has a lazy eye."

"Really? Because the way it followed every pair of ta-tas that entered the room, it seemed to be getting quite the workout to me."

Angie let out a put-upon sigh.

"Change of subject, I get it," Mel said. "Now why did we name our shop Fairy Tale Cupcakes?"

"Because a yummy cupcake is our idea of living happily ever after," Angie said.

"Correct," said Mel. She put a wire whisk and rubber spatula beside each bowl. "Now, who always guarantees a happy ending in a fairy tale?"

"The handsome albeit devoid-of-personality prince?" Angie guessed.

"No."

"Well, it's not the evil stepmother," Angie said. "And the mother is usually dead, so that leaves the furry woodland creatures?"

"No." Mel shook her head. "Come on, think."

"Who's left? The fairy godmother?"

"That's it!"

Angie glanced around the room. "And this works for us how?"

"We'll raffle ourselves off as the lucky winner's fairy godmothers for one day, and we'll call it the Fairy Tale Cupcake Contest."

"Our oven is electric," Angie said. "So you're not suffering brain damage from a gas leak."

"Oh, come on, it's a good idea," Mel said.

"I don't know," Angie said. "I'm not really the fairy godmother type. I'm more the surly dragon who flames people."

"No flaming," Mel said. "I figure we can launch the idea on our website and in a print ad in the *Phoenix New Times.* I'm thinking for every four-pack of cupcakes purchased, the customer can fill out a slip and enter the drawing."

"So, what exactly will we be doing as fairy godmothers?" Angie asked.

"The same thing fairy godmothers always do," Mel said. "Make sure our winner and their date have a fabulous night on the town."

"So, we're talking dinner and transportation?" Angie asked.

"And cupcakes," Mel added.

"How are you planning to pull this off?"

"Simple," she said. "Tate's company has a car service. I'm sure he'll let us use it for one night. And you've heard of the chef Chris Carlisle?"

"The Iron Chef guy over at the Orangewood Resort in Paradise Valley?"

"That's him. Well, he can't make a pie crust to save his life," Mel said. "He would have flunked cooking school if it wasn't for me. He owes me, and I think a romantic dinner for two may pay his bill."

There was a beat of silence while Angie considered her with an expression that was equal parts dismay and admiration.

"I'm not going to be able to talk you out of this, am I?"

Mel paused to consider and then said, "No."

"Fine," Angie said. "I'll check my closet at home and see if I have a pair of fairy wings hanging in there."

"That's my girl." Mel grinned.

The bells on the front door sounded, and they both glanced at the wall clock. Seven o'clock. Time for class.

The Bakersons, Irene and Dan, were the first couple to come in. Mel guessed them to be somewhere in their sixties. Irene wore her gray hair in fat curls all over her head. She was short and sturdy; in fact, she and Dan had similar builds, but where he carried his extra weight hanging low over the front of his belt, Irene carried hers more in the caboose.

What was left of Dan's hair was combed over the large bald spot on the top of his head, fooling no one except himself into thinking he had anything close to a full head of hair. They both wore glasses and track suits, making them look like a matched set. You'd think a couple who chose to spend so much time together would get along better, but no, not these two. They both seemed to have a permanent cantankerous expression etched onto their faces, but only when dealing with one another. Mel could not understand what had possessed them to take her class, but she was too much of a coward to ask.

"You could have had the spot right in

front of the shop, but that would have been too convenient. So now we have to walk a block and a half back to the car, because Mr. Impatient just couldn't wait for anyone to pull out," Irene griped as they entered the kitchen.

Dan looked at his wife, his gaze lingering on her pear shape, and said, "The walk will do you good."

Irene let out a huffy breath, plopped onto a stool, and promptly ignored him.

Three more couples, the Felixes, an elderly pair who lived in town, and the Koslowskis and the Dunns, two senior couples wintering in Scottsdale, arrived, breaking the awkward silence from the Bakersons.

As they filled in the stools around the table, the kitchen door swung wide and the last couple, Jay and Poppy Gatwick, entered. As always, they looked as if they had just walked off the cover of *Vanity Fair*.

Jay had ruddy, masculine good looks and dressed in a Ralph Lauren–at-play style that gave him a grown-up, all-American-boy appeal. Poppy was his perfect complement. She dressed her slender figure in St. John and wore oodles of expensive jewelry, but not the flashy kind. For her it was all black pearls and delicate gold with pavé diamonds, which she slipped off her manicured fingers and tucked into Jay's pocket at the beginning of every class.

The five couples pulled on their student aprons. For the women, it was a paler pink version of the one that Mel and Angie wore, and for the men, it was a nice, macho navy blue. *That is, if a bib apron without barbeque tongs attached can be considered macho,* Mel thought.

Angie disappeared into the walk-in cooler to bring out the tray of cupcakes they'd made earlier. As she set them down in the center of the steel worktable, Mel's students leaned in to study them.

"These are called Kiss Me Cupcakes," Mel said.

"They look yummy," Poppy said. "Don't you think so, Jay?"

"They do, but not nearly as yummy as you." He winked at her. She playfully swatted him, and he grinned.

"How come you never say nice things like that to me?" Irene glared at Dan.

"Maybe if you looked like her I would," he said.

Irene huffed, and Mel pressed on before it got ugly.

"These are mint chocolate chip cupcakes with peppermint buttercream and a Hershey's Kiss on top."

"Oh, I love mint chocolate chip," Candace Dunn said.

"We both do," said her husband. "I bet these don't survive the ride home."

They laughed, and the others joined in. Mel was pleased that she'd picked a winner.

"Let's begin, shall we?"

Mel and Angie circled the tables, instructing the couples and jumping in to help when they needed it. First, they used a whisk to cream together the butter and sugar.

As she watched the couples, Mel saw Mrs. Felix rub the knuckles of her right hand. Mr. Felix patted her shoulder and took over the whisking. Judging by the size of Mrs. Felix's large knuckles, she was suffering from arthritis. Mel knew the Felixes had been married for almost sixty years, and she marveled at the silent communication between them; they really were two halves who made a whole.

"Give me that," Irene snapped at Dan. "You're doing it all wrong."

"I am not!" he protested.

They each had a hand on the handle of their whisk, which was poised to fling butter and sugar all over the room.

"Drop it!" Angie ordered. It was her former elementary school teacher voice, which had been known to bring twenty-five wild second graders to a screeching halt. It worked on adults, too, as was evidenced when both Dan and Irene dropped the whisk and backed away.

Mel retrieved their bowl and tilted it so she could cream together the ingredients and scrape the sides.

"Dan, why don't you finish this?" Mel handed him the bowl. "Just like I was doing. And Irene, why don't you prepare to add the eggs?"

Across the table, she saw Jay with his arms around Poppy as they whisked the batter together. Okay, they were one of those couples who made a person feel queasy with their obvious adoration of one another. But Mel had to admit that mingled in with her gag reflex was a bit of envy. What would it be like to have a man look at her as if she were the center of his universe, the Juliet to his Romeo, like Jay looked at Poppy?

An abrupt banging on the back door drew Mel away from her class. Standing outside the kitchen was her mother, Joyce. Mel crossed the room and unlocked the door.

"Mom, what's up?"

"The ceiling," Joyce quipped.

"Hilarious," Mel said. "Seriously, I'm in the middle of a class. Is everything all right?"

Joyce peeked over Mel's shoulder and finger-waved at the class. They gave amused and confused waves back.

Mel looked closely at her mother. Joyce Cooper never left the house looking less than her best. She was always perfectly made-up and coiffed. She lived by the principle that you never knew what might happen, so you should always look your best, taking the always-wear-clean-underwear thing to a whole new level.

Looking at her now, Mel felt a knot of worry tie up her insides. Joyce's blonde bob was windblown, she had no makeup on, and under her long jacket Mel glimpsed pink thermal pajamas and fuzzy blue slippers.

"Mom, are you ill?" Mel reached up to feel her forehead. It was cool but not clammy.

Angie came scooting over, wearing the same look of concern. "Joyce, are you okay? Should I call urgent care?"

Joyce busted out with a laugh. "I'm fine. Better than fine. I have a date!"

THREE

"What?" Mel staggered backwards until her butt hit a stool and she sat.

"I know, isn't it amazing?" Joyce asked. "But you inspired me. Once you started dating dear Joe, I knew I had to get back out there."

Her mother always called Joe "dear Joe" as if that were his full name. Needless to say, she adored him.

"Mom, this is the first date you've had since . . ."

"I dated your father thirty-five years ago," Joyce finished the sentence. "It's been ten years since he passed. I think it's time. And Baxter — his name is Baxter Malloy — is such a charming man. I just couldn't refuse him."

Mel had often thought her mother should start dating again, but as the years had rolled on and her mother hadn't, Mel had gotten used to the idea that her mom would stay as she was. There was a certain comfort in knowing that she and her brother, Charlie, were her mother's main preoccupations. She wasn't sure how she felt about being usurped.

"Good for you, Joyce," Angie said and stepped around Mel and her stool to give her a hug. Then she elbowed Mel out of her stupor with a whispered "It's just a date — relax."

Angie returned to the students to get them back on task, and Mel shook her head. Angie was right. It was just a date — no biggie. She hopped off of her stool and gave her mother a smile and a hug. "Yeah, good for you, Mom."

Joyce flashed brighter than a motel sign reading VACANCY. Oh, dear.

"I'm so glad you think so," she said. "Well, I don't want to keep you from your class."

"But Mom, where did you meet him?" Mel asked. She didn't want to sound suspicious, but a little more information would not have been out of order.

"It was fate," she said. "You know my friend Ginny?"

"The crazy rich one?" Mel asked.

"Yes, and she's not crazy, she's just impetuous," Joyce said.

"Mom, she thinks she's the secret love

child of Marilyn Monroe and Elvis Presley," Mel said. "She's crackers and not too tightly wrapped."

"Scoff all you want. You never know, she could be," Joyce said. "There is a rumor that they had a secret night together in 1956 and Ginny was born in 1957."

"Moving on," Mel said. She and Joyce had had this debate about Ginny before. Mel liked Ginny, but there was no question she was nuts.

"Well, Ginny invited me out to the Barrett Jackson car auction last week because she wanted to surprise her husband, Monty, with a new car for his birthday."

Mel rolled her hands to signal her mother to speed up the story.

"Well, when it came time to bid, Ginny had to go to the bathroom, so she asked me to do it for her. Well, there were several of us bidding, and then the price got so high that everyone except me and a very distinguished-looking gentleman dropped out. Well, you know Ginny, she never gives in, so I didn't either. I outbid him, and when it was over he came over and kissed my hand and asked for my phone number."

"And you gave it to him?" Mel asked.

"I did!" Joyce said and clapped a hand

over her mouth as if she had surprised herself.

"Let go!" a shrill voice demanded.

Mel glanced over her shoulder. Dan and Irene were arm wrestling over the ice cream scoop they used to fill the cupcake liners with batter. Angie was trying to mediate the situation. The rest of the couples were working together happily. Then her gaze caught Jay Gatwick's. He was frowning at her mother. She supposed Joyce's bedraggled appearance offended his highbrow sensibilities.

Mel turned and walked her mother to the door. "I'd better get back. We'll talk more later. Call me."

"I'll do better than that," Joyce said. "My date is Friday night. That only gives me two days to shop. I'll pick you up tomorrow for lunch and we'll do some shopping. It'll be fun."

They hugged, and Mel watched her mother cross the alley to the parking lot. She waited until Joyce was in her car before she closed and locked the door. When she turned back to the group, Jay was still watching her and looking concerned. Mel gave him a forced smile, and he turned back to his wife.

She supposed in his world of wealth and

position, having someone turn up at your workplace in their pajamas to announce that they had a date was simply not done, which was exactly why she'd left the corporate rat race behind and opened a bakery. She liked keeping the lines between her personal and her professional life blurry.

"Sorry about that," she said as she approached the group. "Mom's a little excited."

"I think it's sweet," Poppy said. "Don't you, darling?"

She glanced at Jay out of the corner of her eye. Mel noticed it was a measuring look, not one of adoration, like she had supposed, but more speculative, as if Poppy were checking to see how much attention Jay was paying to her.

He gave his wife a warm smile. "Very sweet, but not as sweet as you." Poppy looked mollified, and he turned to Mel. "You must be feeling uneasy."

"Why's that?"

"It sounds as if your mother hasn't dated in a while, and she's dating a man you don't know," he said. "What was his name, Baxter something?"

"Malloy. Baxter Malloy. Have you heard of him?" Mel asked.

"No, I can't say that I have," he said.

36

"Well, I have," Mr. Felix said. "He's one of those investment guys. His name is always in the business section of the paper. He's so good at making money that my company invested all of our pensions with him. We're looking at a much more comfortable retirement now."

He and Mrs. Felix exchanged a smile. Mel glanced back at Jay. "Well, that sounds promising."

"It does," Jay said. "Mr. Felix, I had no idea you had such a head for business."

"Oh, I don't," he said with a shake of his head. "I just try to keep up with where my money is going. What about you, Dan? You're an accountant. Have you heard of Baxter Malloy?"

Dan started to splutter and cough, and Irene whacked him on the back. "That's what you get for snitching the Hershey's Kisses."

Red-faced, Dan glared at her, and the rest of the class looked away.

The men started talking finances, but Mel tuned them out to contemplate the bomb her mother had dropped. Joyce had a date with a stranger.

It made Mel feel uneasy, and she wondered if she should have Uncle Stan check Malloy out and how mad her mother would be if she did. *Hmm.* Now she knew how the parents of teenage girls felt. Was there a man good enough for her mother? Not hardly.

Mel stared at the man sprawled out on her futon. His head was tipped back, and soft snores were being emitted from his mouth. He looked as settled in as if he lived there.

Certainly, his clothes were as at home as the rest of him. His red power tie was askew beneath his unbuttoned collar. His charcoal suit jacket was draped over the arm of the foldout bed, and his shoes had wandered off to the other side of her white shag area rug, leaving him plenty of room to stretch out his long legs. For one man, he sure took up a lot of space.

Mel's studio apartment above the shop was just right for her, but when Joe De-Laura showed up, suddenly it felt pinched like a pair of pointy-toed high heels that were two sizes too small.

He had arrived an hour ago with takeout from Pei Wei and a lovely bouquet of tulips. They were yellow with red edges and were now perched in a clear, square glass vase on the counter of her kitchenette. They were lovely. And they almost made up for the fact that he was dead asleep and snoring. Almost.

They had been dating, if you could call it that, for three months. Just after they'd gotten together, the biggest case of Joe's career landed on his desk. As an assistant district attorney, he was prosecuting a serial shooter, and the case was a 24–7 nonstop work-a-thon that didn't leave much time for Mel in his life, unless you counted the amount of time he spent sleeping on her futon.

If she hadn't been half in love with him since she was twelve years old, and if he weren't so darned handsome, she probably would have kicked him to the curb by now, but she just couldn't turn her back on twenty-two years of longing. She was determined to wait it out.

As was becoming her habit, she prepped for lights-out and then rolled him one way and then the other as she made up the bed. The man didn't flutter an eyelid, not even when she took off his tie so he wouldn't strangle himself in his sleep. She snuggled in next to him, and he rolled over and pulled her close. He was solid and warm and, despite the fact that she longed for one or both of them to be naked sometime when they did this, she fell fast asleep.

Mel woke up to the sound of a mug of coffee being plunked onto the table beside her head. There was no better sound in the world. She cracked an eyelid, and there hunched Joe, giving her a wry "there's a crick in my back, but you're worth it" smile that meant more to her than even the tulips he'd brought the night before.

"I fell asleep on you again," he said.

"Hmm," Mel hummed in agreement.

"I'm sorry," he said. "It's this case, it's a . . ."

"Killer," she finished for him. "Sorry, couldn't resist."

He grinned at her. Leaning close, he pulled her into his arms.

"As soon as this case is over, I am whisking you away to a place where no one can find us." He lowered his head and whispered in her ear, "Then I am going to have my way with you . . . repeatedly."

Mel felt her entire body grow hot. "Sounds like a plan." Her voice came out in a froggy croak, and she cleared her throat.

Joe kissed the top of her head and said, "I'll call you later."

She watched him leave and decided he was definitely worth the wait.

"Does this make my butt look big?" Joyce spun around in the three-way mirror at Dillard's, and Mel stifled a yawn. Seven hours, thirteen stores, a number too high to count of rejected outfits, and the beginnings of a blister on her heel, and Joyce had yet to pick a dress for her date. Mel was at her end.

"No, Mom, you look fabulous," she said.

"You're not even looking at me," Joyce chided her. With a miffy humph, she grabbed another selection of outfits, snapped "Excuse me" at a woman in her way, and stomped back into her dressing cubby.

The woman in the way turned and gave Mel an unhappy look. She was standard Scottsdale issue: blonde, buxom, dripping in diamonds, and wearing a body-hugging Dereon animal-print top that showed off her girls to perfection. Mel was willing to bet she'd paid more for her boobs than Mel had for her bakery. Then again, Mel had Tate for financial backing. She glanced at the woman's chest. Yeah, she probably had a financial push-up, too.

"Rude," the woman huffed with a hair toss in Joyce's direction.

Mel frowned. "Didn't I see you in the changing rooms at Nordstrom?"

The woman's eyes widened and then narrowed. "I sincerely doubt it." She scurried into a vacant changing room and slammed the door.

Mel sighed. Obviously she'd been at this too long if she was beginning to think she was seeing the same people at different stores. She took out her cell phone and texted an SOS to her brother Charlie, who lived three hours north in Flagstaff.

Within thirty seconds, her cell phone chimed its distinctive *Gone with the Wind* ringtone.

"Charlie, rent a plane, fly your behind down here, and save me," she said.

"That bad?"

"Worse," she said.

"You just hate shopping," he said. "Man up."

"I have a blister," she whined. "And if I get spritzed by one more department store perfume girl, people are going to start thinking I'm a ho."

"All right, sis," Charlie said. His voice sounded strained, as if he was trying not to laugh. "Here's what you do: When she comes back out, you need to sell her on whatever she's wearing, once and for all."

"I've been trying. Don't you think I've been trying?" Mel's voice came out in a pitch so high she was sure only dogs would be able to hear her.

"It's time for backup," Charlie said. "You need a man. If a man says she looks great, she'll buy whatever she's wearing, even if she looks like a pumpkin."

"I'm in the women's dressing room. Where am I supposed to find a man?"

"Pop your head out and see if there's one of those old guys holding his wife's purse by the door," Charlie said. He always could think on his feet.

"Fine. I'll call you later." Mel ended the call and poked her head out the door, glancing at the cushy seats to the right. Sure enough, three oldsters had been parked with shopping bags and handbags.

The oldest was wearing lime green Bermuda shorts with black socks and loafers. No, Joyce would run for plastic surgery if he told her she looked good. The one in the middle had a waxy sheen to his complexion and was pulling at his ear hairs. No. The third one had thick white hair, sparkling blue eyes, and was dressed in perfectly creased khakis and a Polo golf shirt. Perfect.

Mel sidled up to him. "Hi," she said.

"Hello," he replied.

"Nice day, isn't it?"

"Sure is," he said.

"Mel? Mel, where are you?" her mother called from the dressing room.

So much for the lame cocktail party–type chitchat. Mel needed to get this guy up to

43

speed fast if she ever hoped to see the inside of her bakery again.

"I need a favor," she whispered. "My mother, an older version of me, is about to walk through that door. Please, I beg of you, tell her she is the most beautiful woman you've ever seen."

The man's eyes widened as if he thought Mel was deranged, or maybe his pupils were dilating in reaction to the fog bank of perfume Mel was wearing. Either way, before he could answer, Joyce came strolling out of the dressing room wearing a royal blue designer dress with bolero-style shoulders and three-quarter-length sleeves. Even with mussed hair and chewed-off lipstick, she looked amazing.

"Melanie, I was looking for you," she said.

"Oh, my dear lady," said the man beside Mel as he rose out of his seat and reached for Joyce's hand. "You are a vision."

Joyce's face turned bright pink, and she did a demure half twirl as she put her hand in his. "Do you think so?"

He kissed the back of her hand and leaned back to study her. "You are exquisite."

"Why, thank you," she said.

Suddenly the man reared back and dropped Joyce's hand. One of his hands clutched at his chest while the other fumbled in his pocket.

"Sir?" Mel asked. "Are you all right?"

"My angina," he grunted. "In . . . my . . . pocket . . . my . . . pills."

"Mom, go get help!" Mel said.

Joyce dashed away while Mel helped the man sit down and fished the pills out of his pocket. She unscrewed the top off the prescription bottle and shook a few out with shaky fingers.

"Do you need water?" she asked. He shook his head and opened his mouth. Mel tucked one inside, and he closed his eyes as if waiting for the pill to kick in.

The men in the chairs beside him leaned away as if cardiac arrest might be contagious.

"Henry!" an older woman shrieked from behind Mel. "Henry? Are you all right?"

He patted his chest and gave a nod. Joyce and a clerk came racing back.

"We've called 9-1-1," the clerk said.

The older lady muscled them all out of the way, and as they stood waiting for the paramedic, Mel whispered to her mother, "I suppose you want to get a different dress now?"

"Why would I want to do that?" Joyce asked.

"I don't know, bad juju?"

"Are you kidding me?" she asked. "I gave a man a heart attack in this dress. I'm going to buy one in every color."

"What are we watching?" Mel asked as she strode into Tate's penthouse, shed her jacket, and grabbed a bag of popcorn and a frosty milkshake off the counter.

She plopped down in her usual seat, a recliner to the left of the gigantic flat-screen television he'd had custom built into the wall. It was the first piece of furniture he'd installed in his condominium and vital for their weekly showings of classic movies.

Tate and Angie sat on opposite ends of the big leather couch in the middle. The movie screen was blue, as if they'd been waiting for her to appear before they started, which they probably had, since she had finally finished prepping Joyce for her date and was running a bit late.

"I'll give you a hint," Angie said. " 'Story of my life. I always get the fuzzy end of the lollipop.' "

"*Some Like It Hot,*" Mel said. "Excellent. I could use a screwball comedy."

"What, no Joe tonight?" Tate asked.

"Serial shooter case," Mel said. "I heard the word *depositions* and bailed. He's on his own."

"Too bad," Tate said. "Curtis and Lemmon in drag is a beautiful thing."

Mel noticed Angie watching Tate watching her. Angie suffered from the misguided belief that Tate had a thing for Mel, and Mel had had no luck convincing her otherwise. Now that she was dating Joe, she thought Angie might let go of that whacky notion, but no; Angie was convinced that Tate was jealous of Mel's relationship with Joe.

Mel didn't get that. Tate had sworn off women since his last train wreck of a relationship, and who could blame him? If she'd dated a nut like Christie Stevens, she'd swear off the opposite sex, too.

"And rolling," Tate said as he pressed play.

Mel had finished off her popcorn and was halfway through her box of Whoppers when her phone chimed. Both Angie and Tate gave her dark looks.

"Doesn't Joe know it's movie night?" Angie asked.

Mel glanced at her phone. "It's not Joe. It's my mom."

"Maybe it's a date report," Tate said as he paused the movie. "That guy better be treating her right, or I'll squash him."

Mel flipped open her phone. "Hello?"

"Oh, thank God, you answered," Joyce

47

said breathlessly. "My dress did it again."

"What? What do you mean?"

"My dress," Joyce said. "It caused another heart attack, and this time I think I killed him."

FOUR

"What?"

"Baxter," Joyce said. "He's dead."

"Where are you?" Mel demanded as she sprang to her feet. Tate and Angie watched her, wide-eyed, obviously picking up from her tone that all was not well.

"At his house," she said.

"His house? On a first date?" Mel asked.

Tate jumped up, looking like he was ready to pound someone. Angie was right behind him, looking equally ferocious.

"It's not like it sounds," Joyce said. "The ambulance is here. I have to go."

"Address, Mom. Give me the address," Mel said.

"Oh, I'm not sure, it's the big house on Saguaro Road, just past Forty-second Street," she said.

"I'll be there in ten minutes, and I'm calling Uncle Stan," Mel said.

"What's going on?" Angie asked as they

followed Mel to the elevator.

"Mom's date is dead," she said.

"Holy . . ." Tate began.

"Crap," Angie finished.

"My car is faster. I'll drive," Tate said.

Mel looked at her hands. They were shaking.

"Good idea."

Tate jetted his silver Lexus across town. They peeled up a winding hill, rolled through three stop signs, and came to a screeching halt in front of a mansion that was nestled on the north side of Camelback Mountain. The estates were many here in Paradise Valley, but it was easy to pick out the one they were looking for, as three police cars and an ambulance were parked out front with lights flashing. Not exactly balloons signaling a kid's birthday party, but it would do.

Mel shoved open her door and started to run. Several uniformed officers were standing in her way, but she raced around them, frantically searching the sparse crowd for signs of her mother's blonde bob.

"Mom!" she called. "Mom!"

The large double doors to the glass-and-stone mansion stood wide open, so Mel charged through the entrance with Tate and Angie on her heels.

She ignored the black tile and glass furniture and the precisely lit objets d'art. All she wanted was to find Joyce safe and sound.

She noticed that a crowd had gathered on the back patio by the pool. She made a beeline. As soon as she stepped through the glass doors at the back, however, a hand grabbed her elbow and brought her up short.

"Authorized personnel only," the officer said.

Mel yanked her elbow out of his hand. "I am authorized. I'm with the DA's office. These are my assistants."

Okay, technically she was sleeping, literally, with a person in the DA's office, so it wasn't a total lie, or so she told herself. The officer released her elbow and stepped back. Well, hello. It worked.

She strode forward, past the outdoor fireplace, the granite cooking area, the barbeque pit, and the built-in lounge. She circled the dark blue–tile swimming pool, which with its interior lighting cast the area in an eerie blue glow.

A short stairway led up to a sunken hot tub. And there, in the middle of a knot of uniforms, huddled in a patio chair, sat Joyce. She was bundled in a standard-issue

51

gray police blanket. Her hair looked wet and her makeup streaked. Even from twenty feet away, Mel could see her shivering.

The minute she saw Mel, Joyce rose to her feet, looking ready to sob with relief. Mel folded her mother in her arms and held her tight.

"Are you all right?" she asked.

"I'm fine," Joyce said, although her teeth were chattering, and she felt icy cold to the touch.

"Excuse me, ma'am," a man said. "We have some more questions."

Mel clamped her mother to her side and spun to face the officer. He was several inches taller than her, wearing khakis and a dress shirt, the uniform of a detective. She could see the badge clipped at his waist and the shoulder holster that housed his gun. His short brown hair was combed back from his face, giving him a stern demeanor. Mel didn't care.

"My mother is standing here shivering. She is going to warm up and dry off and then she'll be happy to answer your questions," she said.

The detective narrowed his gaze at her. "Who the hell are you?"

"Joe DeLaura's girlfriend," she said.

"And I'm his sister," Angie chimed in.

"I'm neither," Tate said. "But I play a mean game of golf."

The detective glowered at them. It was obvious he could not care less who they were dating or were related to or what their golf handicaps were. When it looked as if he was about to open his mouth and yell, he was interrupted by a new arrival.

"Detective Martinez," Uncle Stan said as he held out his hand. "Detective Cooper, Scottsdale PD."

"A bit out of your jurisdiction, isn't it?" Martinez asked as they shook.

Uncle Stan gestured to Mel and Joyce. "Family."

Martinez gave him a curt nod. "Dry her off, but she doesn't leave until I say."

"Thanks," Uncle Stan said. He put his arm around Joyce and led her back to the outside fireplace, which was ablaze.

Mel, Angie, and Tate followed. Mel went to pull the sodden blanket off her mother's shoulders, but Joyce only clutched it tighter.

"Mom, we need to dry you off. You're going to catch pneumonia."

"I can't take it off," Joyce whispered.

"Why not?"

Joyce lowered her head and mumbled.

"I didn't catch that," Mel said.

Joyce sighed. "I can't take it off. I'm in

my underwear."

She flashed Mel a shot of her blue bra strap, and Mel gasped.

"Mom!"

"What?"

"On a first date?" Mel asked. "I am shocked!"

"It's not how it looks," Joyce said. "We were going to jump in the hot tub."

"Hot tub?" Mel slapped a hand to her forehead.

"Don't be such a prude," Joyce chided her. "I went into the cabana to hang up my dress and borrow a robe, and when I came out, Baxter was floating facedown in the pool."

"Good grief," Tate muttered. "Did he fall in and hit his head?"

"No, I think it was the dress," Joyce said in an ominous voice. "I think it's cursed."

"Mom, it's not the dress," Mel said. "It's just a freak accident."

"Joyce," Uncle Stan interrupted, "did you see or hear anyone on the premises?" He had his cop face on. His usual affectionate expression was gone, lost behind the hard angles and planes of a face that had spent too much time catching bad people making bad decisions and telling bad lies. His worldview was just all-around bad.

54

"No, there was no one," Joyce said. Her teeth clacked together, and she pulled the blanket tighter. "I thought he was swimming at first, then I thought he was joking, then I realized he was in trouble, and I jumped in and fished him out. I called 9-1-1, and I tried to do CPR, but he was already gone. That's when I called you, Melanie."

"Mel, go get your mother's clothes," Uncle Stan said. "I'm going to talk to Martinez and see how much longer they're going to need you."

Joyce reached out and clutched his hand. "Thanks, Stan."

The hard lines disappeared. Uncle Stan's face was once again filled with gentleness, and he leaned forward and placed a kiss on Joyce's head. "It's going to be all right."

Mel hurried across the patio towards the cabanas. They were four small changing rooms built into the side of the house just beyond the hot tub.

A knot of police, including Martinez, a photographer, and a medical examiner, were near that end of the pool. Mel knew they were gathered around Baxter Malloy's body. And just like at the scene of an accident on the highway, she felt herself slowing down, rubbernecking, to get a look-see at the man her mother had been out with.

She saw a shock of white hair over a very tan face — unnaturally tan, in fact. He was splayed out on his back with his arms wide. He was still clothed, thank heavens, from his dress shirt and slacks to his loafers. Obviously, he hadn't gone into the pool by choice, then.

She felt a pair of eyes watching her, and she glanced up to see Detective Martinez studying her. He was younger than she had first realized and handsome, too, in a testosterone laden "I put away bad guys" sort of way.

Her toes hit the bottom step of the stairs that led up to the cabanas, and she broke eye contact with the detective in order to stop herself before she tripped. She failed and had to catch herself on the steps, narrowly escaping a full splat against the hard stones. Grace in motion, hardly.

When Mel glanced back up from her stooped position, Martinez was watching her, and he looked amused. She pushed herself into an upright position and felt her face get hot with embarrassment. She stomped up the stairs. Served her right for gawking at a dead man, she supposed.

She found her mother's blue dress on a hanger in a tiny closet in the second cabana. Her shoes had been carefully placed on the floor beneath the dress. Joyce was always tidy; even at someone else's house there was a place for everything and everything in its place.

She took the dress and shoes and trotted back to the fireplace. When she got there, Detective Martinez was holding a large brown envelope and a small notepad and was asking her mother questions while Uncle Stan hovered protectively behind her.

"Can you identify this, Mrs. Cooper?" he asked.

Mel saw Detective Martinez hold out a clear plastic bag containing one nude thigh-high stocking with lace-trimmed edges.

"Oh, that's mine," Joyce said.

"Can you explain how this came to be in Mr. Malloy's pocket?" he asked.

Joyce's face turned a shade of red only found on small, bitter root vegetables.

"I, uh, we . . ." she stammered. She glanced skyward as if hoping a meteor might plummet to Earth at that very second and spare her this conversation. Mel glanced up, too. Clear sky. No such luck.

With a heavy sigh, Joyce said, "We were playing shoe salesman, and Baxter took my stockings off for me."

It was safe to say every single person in the group was now hoping for a meteor to hit. Tate cleared his throat. Uncle Stan puffed out his cheeks. Angie and Mel exchanged glances of equal parts *wow* and *ew*. The noted exception was Detective Martinez, who looked unfazed, as if he heard worse than this every day.

"Can I get dressed now?" Joyce asked.

Martinez looked up from the pad on which he was making notes. "Yes."

"Thank you," Joyce said. Mel handed her the dress and shoes.

"One thing," Martinez said.

"Yes?" Joyce asked, looking wary.

"We only found one of your stockings on his person," he said. "What happened to the other one?"

"I don't know," she answered, looking pained. "He had both of them when I went to change."

"Interesting," Martinez said.

"How so?" Uncle Stan asked.

"The medical examiner seems to think Mr. Malloy didn't just have a heart attack and fall into the pool," he said. "In fact, it appears he was strangled by this."

Martinez produced another baggie with a stocking in it from inside the large brown envelope. This one was wet and left droplets of water in the bag.

"We found this one in the pool. His assailant must have dropped it after killing him," Martinez said.

Joyce gasped and then keeled over with a thud.

FIVE

"Shoe salesman, Mom? Really?" Mel asked as she drove her mother home.

"It was fun," Joyce sniffed. She held an ice pack that one of the ambulance guys had given her over the knot on her forehead. "You have to remember, I haven't dated in thirty-five years. How am I supposed to know what to do?"

Mel sighed. Obviously, she had let her mother go out woefully unprepared.

"Fair enough," she said. "Just promise me if that if one of your dates ever pulls out a video camera, you'll run. I don't think I'm up for an X-rated film of my mother being circulated on the Internet."

Joyce looked at her in horror. "That's it. I'm never dating again."

Mel thought about talking her out of it, but something stopped her. She had a guilty feeling it was relief.

She pulled up in front of the house her

mother had lived in for over thirty years. Nestled in the Arcadia neighborhood with a lovely view of Camelback Mountain, it was an old, low-slung ranch that boasted a large yard and several of the original orange trees. Mel walked her mother up the cobbled path to the front door.

A sedan pulled into the drive. It was Uncle Stan. Watching him stride up the drive reminded Mel so much of her father that she felt an ache in her chest. Uncle Stan was robust like his older brother had been and had the same "taking a room by storm" sort of walk. The Cooper men were not the type to be ignored. But where Charlie Cooper, Mel's father, had been found frequently chomping the soggy end of a cigar and telling bawdy jokes, Stan popped antacids, grinding them between his molars like sidewalk chalk under a bicycle tire, quietly watching the world at large, suspecting everyone was up to no good.

"Do you want me to spend the night, Mom?" Mel asked.

"No, I'm fine, dear," Joyce said. "You needn't trouble yourself. You have a shop to run."

"It's no trouble," Mel protested, but Uncle Stan cut in. "Don't worry, Mel. I'll stay the night in the guesthouse. You don't happen to have the fixings for an omelet, do you, Joyce?"

"I do," she said. "Mushrooms and cheese?"

"That'd be nice." He smiled at her.

A look of understanding passed between them that made Mel feel like a child trying to grasp an adult conversation. She suspected they both knew that Mel's company would not make Joyce feel as safe as Stan's would, but neither of them wanted to offend her by saying as much.

"I'll just go change into my pajamas and robe and meet you in the kitchen," Joyce said. She kissed Mel's cheek on the way to her room. "Thanks for coming to get me. I'll call you tomorrow."

Uncle Stan walked Mel out to her car.

"Don't worry," he said. "I'll keep an eye on her."

"Thanks," she said. He opened his arms, and she stepped into them. He wrapped her in a huge bear hug that somehow made her feel like everything was going to be okay, even as it made her miss her dad all the more.

Mel arrived home to find Joe sitting on the steps that led up to her apartment.

"Angie called me," he said. He gave her a

quick hug and stepped back to study her. "Are you okay? Is your mom okay?"

"She . . . I . . . we're fine," Mel said. "What a crazy night."

She walked up the stairs to her apartment with Joe following. Once inside she dropped her purse, kicked off her shoes, and landed on the futon with a thump.

Joe sat down beside her and pulled her close. "You know you could have called me."

"It didn't seem right," Mel said. "It was all very odd with Mom being in her underwear, and Uncle Stan was there. I didn't want to bother you."

"You had no problem saying you were with me to the police," he said. He sounded irritated. "We're dating. It's no bother."

Mel glanced at him and felt a spurt of annoyance. His short black hair was mussed, his tie was askew, and the cuffs on his dress shirt were rolled back to his elbows. It was closer to Saturday morning than Friday night, and he looked as if he'd just come from the office. In fact, she was sure he had just come from his office. The man was a workaholic, and he wondered why she hesitated to call him?

"We're not dating," she argued, feeling cranky. "We're roomies on nights you drag your sorry carcass over here and pass out.

My mother was half naked and playing shoe salesman. I think she went further on her first date than we have in months. Is it really any wonder I didn't call you?"

Joe frowned at her. By birth order, he was smack dab in the middle of Angie's seven older brothers. A smart kid, he had turned that spot into his niche, always being the sibling mediator, the peacemaker, the one everyone turned to with their troubles. Really, it had surprised no one when he became a lawyer. He liked to be the fixer. He liked to be needed. He did not like to think he was blowing it big time.

"Shoes? Would that do it for you?" he asked. He looked at her sock-clad feet. "I could probably get one of those metal foot-measuring things on eBay."

He wiggled his eyebrows, and Mel had to press her lips together to keep from laughing.

"You're missing the point," she said, trying to maintain her ire and failing spectacularly.

"Listen," he said, "I know the case I've been working on really came at a bad time for us, but it's almost over."

Mel looked at him. She'd heard this before. She untangled herself from him and rolled off the couch. She crossed the room to the door.

"Tell you what, Joe: When your case is over, call me," she said.

He stood. "Are we breaking up?"

"There isn't anything to break up," Mel said. " 'I think what we got on our hands is a dead shark.' "

"Alvy Singer in *Annie Hall*," Joe said, identifying the quote. He moved to stand in front of her. "Our shark isn't dead. Hell, he hasn't even had a chance to get in the pool."

He pulled Mel into his arms and planted a kiss on her that made her knees buckle. How did he do that?

"I'm not giving up on us, Cupcake, and neither should you. I'll call you tomorrow."

Mel closed the door behind him and couldn't figure out if they'd just broken up or not. She suspected not. And suddenly, that was okay. Any man who could nail a line from *Annie Hall* deserved another chance.

Besides, given the evening she'd had, she wasn't sure she was in a proper emotional state to declare the status of any relationship.

Tate strolled into Lo-Lo's Chicken and Waffles with the Sunday paper tucked under his arm. Angie and Mel sat at their usual

65

table, waiting for him. Lo-Lo's was a Phoenix landmark known for the best fried chicken and red velvet cake in the state. Mel had been thrilled when they opened up a second restaurant just down the road from the bakery. As usual the place was mobbed, and Tate had to throw a few elbows to get to his seat.

Angie had already ordered him a Lo-Lo's, which consisted of three pieces of chicken, southern style, and two waffles. Mel and Angie had lesser versions of the same, as they always saved room for Sanny Sand's red velvet cake. They each had a large sweet tea to wash it all down.

"So, how is Mom doing?" Tate asked Mel as he sat down and tucked into his food.

"Shaky," Mel said. She gave him a pained look. "Apparently Detective Martinez asked my mother if Baxter was into eroto-asphyxiation, and Uncle Stan almost punched him in the face."

Both Tate and Angie cringed.

"Then, of course, Uncle Stan had to explain what that is to Mom, which gave her a fit of hysterics."

"I'm assuming they've ruled that out then?" Tate asked, wiping his mouth with his napkin before taking up another piece of chicken.

"Yes, so far it looks as if they believe Mom was just an innocent bystander, but until they come up with another suspect, she's on the hot seat. I get the feeling they would really love it if she could just remember seeing someone else there that night."

"Do they have any other suspects?" Angie asked.

"Uncle Stan said Malloy's son is in town and that the police are questioning him as well."

"Was there bad blood between them?" Tate asked.

"I don't know." Mel took a bite of her chicken and almost swooned. It was crispy and crunchy and seasoned to perfection.

"Well, after you told me what Mr. Felix said about his company investing all of their pensions with Malloy's company, I did some checking in investment circles," Tate said. "I knew I had heard the name Baxter Malloy. He used to live on the East Coast and was a big trader. There were a lot of rumors about him, however, that something wasn't quite right."

"Can you find out more?" Mel asked.

"I've already put my feelers out," Tate said.

The rest of lunch passed in silent, chewing appreciation of Lo-Lo's, with the occasional debate about what to view for their next movie night. Angie was lobbying for a romantic comedy, since Valentine's Day was rapidly approaching. Mel was hankering for an over-the-top Carmen Miranda musical, like she always did in times of stress. Tate was favoring any of Clint's classic spaghetti Westerns.

"So what we need is a singing, 'fruit basket on the head' heroine, falling in love with a funny hero, while they ride off into the sunset together having gutshot a bunch of bad guys," Tate said.

"That'd do it," Angie said.

"I'll see what I can come up with," he said.

As they lingered over their sweet tea and red velvet cake, Tate handed out sections of the newspaper. Mel took the Life section first. She scanned an article about teeth care and then turned the page. Her heart stopped in her throat. "Oh, fudge!" she said.

Six

"What? What is it?" Tate and Angie asked together.

Mel flipped the paper open so they could see. On a quarter-page in bold pink was their advertisement for the Fairy Tale Cupcake Contest. For every four-pack of cupcakes purchased, customers could enter a drawing to win a night on the town, courtesy of Fairy Tale Cupcakes.

"In all of the hullabaloo I completely forgot," she said.

"Me, too," Angie moaned.

"You have to go through with it now," Tate said. "Besides, it's not that much work. All you have to do is sell cupcakes and fill that raffle box. The dinner is all set and so is the car. It'll be fine."

"I hope you're right," Mel said. "My heart is really not in it right now."

"No, but just imagine Olivia Puckett's face when she picked up the paper this morning. I bet she about had a stroke," Angie said.

"I can rally for that," Mel said.

"Thought you might," Angie said. "Come on. If we're kicking this off tomorrow, like we say in the ad, we have to get to the shop and get some work done."

"Right behind you," Mel said. They hugged Tate goodbye and hurried out of Lo-Lo's and back to the bakery.

It was a quiet afternoon at Fairy Tale Cupcakes. A few tourists popped in wanting individual cupcakes, and Angie took two phone orders for cupcakes for the next week, but otherwise all was quiet.

Mel decided they'd better come up with a raffle box for the contest, so she took some leftover silver wrapping paper and a large cardboard box she'd been hoarding in her office for just this sort of thing. She had just finished covering the box with the silver paper when the front door banged open, shoved with more force than necessary, by an angry-looking man. He was tall and lanky, dressed in jeans and a flowing white shirt with a thread count that was so low she could see the ink of the many tattoos covering his arms through the fabric. He had long, straight black hair, a hook in his nose as if it had been broken repeatedly, full

70

lips over a stubborn chin, and piercing pale blue eyes. He was attractive in a bad-boy, "your mom would have a coronary if you brought him home" kind of way.

He did not look like a lover of cupcakes, or anything else sweet, for that matter. In fact, Mel would place odds that he was a salt guy. He stalked across the room, stopping by the booth where she was finishing the box.

"May I help you?" she asked.

He looked her over with an insolence that crossed the border into rudeness.

"That depends," he said. His upper lip curled slightly in what would have been an attractive, Elvis-like sneer if it hadn't carried a butt-load of hostility with it. "Are you Ms. Cooper?"

"Yes, I am," she said. She tried to place him. Had they met before? Did he have a reason to be mad at her? Had she cut anyone off while driving lately? Or worse, had she dated him at some point and forgotten?

She glanced at his face. No, she'd remember those eyes. Although he did look familiar, she just couldn't figure out why.

"You're a little young for him, don't you think?"

"Excuse me?" she asked.

"But then, that makes sense doesn't it?" he asked.

"No, actually, I have no idea what you're talking about," she said.

Angie came through the swinging doors from the kitchen with a tray full of Death by Chocolate Cupcakes for the display case. She plopped the tray on the counter and glanced over at Mel and the man with the bad attitude.

"Need help?" she asked.

The man glowered at her. "Tell your friend her little plan won't work."

Angie glanced at Mel. "Your little plan won't work." Then she looked back at the man. She cocked her head and studied him. "Just to clarify, what plan would that be?"

"To get away with murdering my father," he said. He glared at Mel. "I heard the old man was running around with a blonde."

Mel opened her mouth to protest, but he gave her a scathing head-to-toe sweep with his eyes. "I don't know what you have to gain by killing an old man, but I plan to find out."

Mel felt her eyes pop, but she was rendered temporarily speechless from sheer shock. Angie, however, was not.

"What are you talking about?" she snapped.

She did not have seven older brothers for nothing. Virtually no one and nothing ever intimidated her. She stomped around the counter and, despite her diminutive stature, she managed to get right under the angry man's nose and give him what for. "Who do you think you are, coming into our place of business and accusing one of us of murder? Why I ought to . . ."

She paused to look for a weapon and, in a show of good sense, the angry man backed up a few steps. Not that it helped him any as, unable to latch on to a suitable weapon, Angie pursued, keeping her face inches from his chest while she jabbed him in the belly with her pointer finger.

"Apologize, you big dummy, and make it quick, because I am losing my patience!"

The man raised his hands in surrender and looked at Angie as if she were the most marvelous thing he'd ever seen.

"I . . . I'm . . . sorry," he stammered. "The police said Ms. Cooper was with my father when he died. After they got done questioning me, I just lost it. I called information, and they gave me this address."

"Is that the best you can do?" she challenged.

"I am very sorry," he said, looking over Angie's head at Mel. "Please forgive me."

"You're Baxter Malloy's son?" Mel asked.

"Yes," he said.

Mel stepped forward and put her hand on Angie's shoulder, easing her back from the man. "He just lost his father," she said. "Let's give him a break."

Angie squinted at him and finally muttered, "Okay."

"Would you like to sit down?" Mel asked.

The man nodded and slid into an empty booth. His rage was gone, leaving him looking bewildered. Mel knew how it felt to lose a father, and she couldn't help but feel sorry for him, even if he had wrongly accused her of being involved.

"Can I offer you a cupcake?" she asked.

"Thanks, but I'm not really a sweets guy," he said.

Mel nodded. She'd figured.

"How about a glass of iced tea, unsweetened?" Angie offered. She looked as if it pained her to do so.

The man smiled at her, and the grin transformed his face into one of pure charm. Again, Mel felt sure she had seen him somewhere before. "Thanks, that would be great."

Angie went to the kitchen, and Mel took the seat across from him.

"I'm Mel Cooper," she said and extended

her hand. "My mother is Joyce Cooper. She's the one who had a date with your father."

He shook her hand, looking chagrinned. "Oh, I really did step in it, didn't I?"

"Barefoot," Mel confirmed.

Angie returned to the booth with a tray of three iced teas. She slid in beside Mel.

"I'm Brian Malloy," he said. He held out his hand to Angie, who took it grudgingly.

"Angie DeLaura," she said. "I'm sorry for your loss."

"Thank you," he said. "Honestly, my father and I were not close. He didn't approve of my life, and I thought his was . . . well, I guess I didn't approve of his, either. It made for some tense family holidays until we finally scrapped the whole thing after my mother died. I moved to Los Angeles three years ago, and we haven't spoken since."

"I'm sorry," Angie said.

Mel glanced at her and realized that her sympathy was heartfelt. Angie was all about family. Her brothers drove her crazy, but she'd take a bullet for any one of them and vice versa. Angie always felt badly for people who didn't have that unconditional love in their families.

"Me, too," Mel said. A thought wriggled

in the corner of her mind, however, and she had to ask. "How is it you're here now if you live in Los Angeles?"

"Quite a coincidence, isn't it?" Brian said. He tossed his long black hair back over his shoulder with a humorless laugh. "The police really loved that one. But the fact is, I'm on tour, and I'm just passing through. I was in rehearsal for our gig at the time of his death."

Angie sat bolt upright. "Oh! Now I recognize you. You're Roach! You're the drummer in the band the Sewers. I love you guys.

"Na na na. Na na na. Step on this! Yeah, step on this! Like this? Yeah!" Angie sang with a mean air guitar riff. Unfortunately, Angie was not known for her singing.

Brian gave her a small smile. "Thanks."

An awkward silence filled the booth. Now that Angie and Mel knew they were sitting with a celebrity, it felt different. Roach took a long sip from his glass while Mel and Angie stared at him, trying to process the information that they were sitting with someone who had three platinum albums and was on a world tour.

"Well, I guess I'd better get back to the hotel. Our manager wants me to do a press conference about my dad's murder, something about damage control."

"Oh, yes, of course," they said. As one, they rose and followed him to the door.

Roach grabbed the door handle and said, "Thanks for the iced tea."

"Any time, we're open from ten to eight every day but Sunday, which is one to five, but you can probably read that on the door." Mel stammered to a halt, and Angie gave her a look that told her quite plainly she sounded like an idiot. She clamped her lips shut.

"Hey," Roach said, looking at Angie, "if I leave a ticket for tomorrow night's show at the box office, will you come?"

"Can I have three?" Angie asked with a grin.

"Will you have dinner with me after?" he asked.

She studied him for a second. "Yes."

"Then you can have as many as you want," he said.

"Three will do," she said.

"See you tomorrow night," he said.

The door shut behind him, and Mel goggled at Angie.

"Did you really just accept a date with a rock star?" she asked.

"Yes, I think I did."

"What about Tate?" Mel asked.

Angie walked back to the counter where

she'd left her tray of Death by Chocolates. She started putting them into the display case.

"What about him?" she asked as Mel followed her and began to help.

"I thought you were in love with him," she said.

"I am, but he's not in love with me, and he probably never will be," Angie said. "I need to move on."

"With a guy named Roach?"

"That's his nickname," Angie said. "Besides, he's hot. You have to admit, he's hot."

"So? Don't you find it the least bit odd that he just happens to be on tour in town when his father is murdered? He even admitted that they had a strained relationship. Angie, he could be a murderer!" Mel said. "You can't date him. I forbid it."

SEVEN

Angie's face took on a ferocity that in twenty-plus years of friendship Mel had never had turned upon her. It was wet-your-pants scary, and she wished more than anything that she could bite back the words that had just escaped her lips.

"Don't tell me what to do," Angie said. The words were even more intimidating because they were said quietly.

Mel raised her hands. "My bad. Sorry. You're right. It's your life. I'm just concerned because I love you."

In a blink, Angie's face softened, and she reached out and hugged Mel.

"I'm sorry," she said. "You know how crazy I get when someone tries to boss me around. Thirty-four years of living with the brothers will do that to a gal."

"It's okay," Mel said. "I was out of line."

"You're my best friend," Angie said. "You're never out of line. And you don't need to worry. If I get any crazy murderer vibe off of him, I'll dump him flat."

Mel stared at her hard.

"What?"

"I don't like this."

"It's just dinner."

"So was my mother's date with his father," Mel said.

"Mel, relax. I'll be fine. Now, bigger picture — it's a free concert, and I scored tickets for you and Tate, too, so how cool am I?"

"Pretty cool," Mel admitted with a smile.

Mel's phone began to ring its distinctive *Gone with the Wind* ringtone. She fished it out of her apron pocket and glanced at the screen. It was her mom.

"Hi, Mom, how are you?"

"I need you to come over and take away the dress," Joyce said.

"The dress?" Mel asked.

"Yes, I am sure it's cursed. It's killed two men already. I can't let it kill another."

"Mom, the man at Dillard's didn't die, and the medical examiner said Baxter was strangled," she said. "He didn't have a heart attack. It had nothing to do with the dress."

"You don't know that," she insisted. "Please, I need you to come and get the dress."

"What do you want me to do with it? Take it to Goodwill?"

"Oh, goodness no," Joyce said. "Then some poor unsuspecting person will suffer the curse. No, you have to destroy it."

"Will you feel better if I do?"

"Yes," Joyce sighed.

"Okay, then I'll come over after work and get it."

"Thank you."

"Anytime," Mel said.

Angie looked at her with raised eyebrows.

"I have to get rid of 'the dress,' " she said.

"Makes sense," Angie agreed.

Of course it made sense to Angie. She was Italian and had a very healthy superstitious streak running through her. If her palms itched, she was convinced she was going to have good luck. She even wore an amethyst pendant of her grandmother's to ward off the *malocchio,* the evil eye.

"No, it doesn't," Mel said. "It's just my mother being weird. Malloy didn't die because of her dress."

"How do you know?" Angie asked. "It could be cursed."

Mel rolled her eyes and picked up the finished raffle box and placed it prominently on the front counter. They would run the raffle for one week. That should give them plenty of entrants for the drawing.

The front door was pushed open, and in shuffled an older gentleman. Mel looked more closely. No, there was nothing merely "older" about him. This guy was a fossil. She was only surprised he didn't leave a trail of dust behind him when he walked.

His back curved like a question mark, leaving him significantly shorter than he'd most likely been a half century before. He wore dark pants that were hitched a bit too high by a pair of wide, red suspenders. His shirt was white with thin blue stripes, buttoned up to the collar and covered in a thin cardigan sweater in nondescript beige. He wore gold-rimmed glasses that slid low on his nose, and his hair . . . well, it was more of a removable hair hat in a shade of reddish brown that his head had not produced on its own in at least thirty years.

"Good afternoon, sir," Angie greeted him. "May I help you?"

The man shuffled forward in his orthopedic shoes and smacked the newspaper down on the counter. "I want to enter the contest."

"Well, it doesn't actually start until tomorrow," Angie said.

"I might be dead tomorrow," the old man grumped.

"He has a point," Mel said. "I think we can let him enter today."

"Okay," Angie said. "When you buy a four-pack of cupcakes, you get an entry form, and you can fill it out and put it right in that box. What four cupcakes would you like?"

"How should I know?" he snapped. "What do you have?"

Angie looked over her shoulder at Mel, who shrugged. It had been long established that Angie was the cranky magnet. It never failed that if a cranky person came in, he went right to Angie.

"What's that one?" he asked as he tapped the glass of the display case.

"This one?" Angie asked, pointing to a Death by Chocolate.

"No, the other one," he said. His tone made it clear that he didn't think she was very bright.

"That's our Blonde Bombshell," she said. "It's an almond cupcake . . ."

"Then why is it pink?" he asked.

"It's not pink," she said.

"Then it's not the one I'm asking about," he said. "What's the pink one?"

"That's called a Tinkerbell," Angie said.

"Stupid name," he grumbled.

Angie took a deep breath through her nose

and kept going. "It's a lemon cupcake with a raspberry buttercream frosting."

"Give me four," he said.

"Okay, then," she said. Angie reached below the counter to get a box, but he stopped her.

"I don't need a box," he said. "I'm going to eat them here."

"All four?" she asked.

"Yep," he said. "And don't forget my entry form."

"Certainly," Angie said. "Anything to drink?"

"Water," he said.

The man filled out the form with a shaky hand while Angie rang up his order. He handed it to Mel and asked, "Can you read it?"

The writing resembled spider tracks, but it was still legible.

"Yes, Mr. Zelaznik," she said. "I can read it."

"Good," he said. "I have a hot mama I've been planning to ask out, and your contest is just the ticket to show her a good time."

Angie and Mel exchanged a glance and then Mel turned back with a smile. "Well, good luck."

She tucked his form into the box while Angie took his tray to a nearby booth. Mr.

Zelaznik trailed after her, easing into the booth as if he were afraid he might fall and be stuck on his back like a turtle on its shell.

Two hours later, Mr. Zelaznik was still in his booth. The Sunday afternoon tourist crush had come and gone, and still he sat working on his sixteenth cupcake.

"Do you think he might go into sugar shock?" Angie asked. "I love sweets more than anyone, but even I'd throw up if I ate that many cupcakes in one sitting."

Mr. Zelaznik looked red-faced and sweaty. His hair hat was askew, and his eyes were becoming glassy. Mel was worried he'd had a four-pack too many.

"Maybe we should call him a cab," she said to Angie. She had locked the front door and flipped the hanging sign on the front window to CLOSED.

"Mr. Zelaznik," she said. "It's time to go home."

He looked at her, but she could tell he hadn't heard a word she'd said.

"Mr. Zelaznik, put down the fork!" Angie barked in her schoolteacher voice.

He dropped his fork and blinked at them.

"You know, you don't have to eat the cupcakes all at once," she said. "You could take some home and share them with a friend."

"Nah," he grumped. "I don't want anyone to know what I'm doing. They'll steal my idea."

He shuffled out of the booth. Mel was encouraged to see he was moving faster than when he came in, but that could be all the sugar coursing through his bloodstream.

"Would you like us to call a ride for you?" she asked.

"Nah," he refused. "The trolley will take me right to my house."

"If you're sure," she said.

Angie dumped her apron and grabbed her purse from the back room.

"I'm going to follow him to make sure he gets home okay," she said.

"Good idea," Mel said. "See you tomorrow."

Mel locked up the bakery, cleaning as she made her way to the back. It was just after five, and she still needed to get to her mother's to collect "the dress." Suddenly, she wanted nothing more than to climb up the back stairs to her apartment, put on her jammies, curl up in bed, and watch all the episodes of *Inspector Lewis* she had saved on her DVR.

As she locked up the bakery and walked to her car, she flipped open her phone and sent a text to her brother, Charlie. He was coming down this week to be with their mom. She told him to call her when he arrived. It was good to have backup.

She drove over to her mother's house. She parked in the wide driveway, and before she was even halfway up the walk, the door opened and her mother came steaming down the cobbled path towards her. In her hand she held a Dillard's bag, which she thrust into Mel's arms.

"Take it," Joyce said. She turned her head dramatically to the side, very Bette Davis. "I never want to see it again."

Mel flung the bag into the back of her car.

"Have you eaten?" Joyce asked, her inner drama queen being squashed by her more common role of ever-vigilant, worried mother.

"Depends," Mel said. "What do you have?"

"Uncle Stan just left, but I made us sloppy joes and Tater Tots, and I have plenty of both left."

"Tots?" Mel asked. "I'm in."

Mel sat at the counter in her mother's kitchen. The high-back stools were the same ones she'd sat on as a kid. She took the one on the right, because she always sat on the right, and noticed that it still wobbled, because one leg was shorter than the other three.

Mel had been a chunky kid, and one of the brackets on the bottom of the stool had broken off when she sat down too heavily one day. She'd cried for an hour and then eaten an entire bag of Doritos.

She remembered doing her homework at this counter with Charlie beside her, the two of them sharing a plate of cookies while Joyce cooked dinner and grilled them about school. Back then, the counter had been white Formica with tiny gold flecks. Now it was brown-and-gray granite. It was colder to the touch than she remembered and, suddenly, she longed for the old Formica.

She missed it like she missed the feeling of absolute safety she'd had as a child. No matter what happened, it would be okay because her mother and father were there to take care of things. All of that had changed ten years ago when her father had died. Sometimes she was shocked by how much she still missed him.

"What are you thinking about?" Joyce asked as she slid a plate and a glass of milk in front of Mel.

Somehow a small side salad had appeared on the plate next to the Tots and the hamburger bun filled with sloppy joe. Mel smiled. That was so like her mother, bribing her with Tots and sneaking in a salad.

"I'm thinking that I'm lucky to have you, Mom," she said.

Joyce teared up and patted her hand. "I miss your dad, too."

Mel decided to change the subject before they both got soggy. "Is Charlie coming alone, or is he bringing Nancy and the boys?"

"They're all coming," Joyce said. She sounded happy, and Mel was relieved to see the familiar sparkle light her eyes. Joyce loved her grandsons.

They spent the rest of Mel's mealtime making plans for the boys, and then Mel gave her mom a big squeeze good-bye.

"What are you going to do with it?" Joyce asked as they walked out the door. Mel knew she meant "the dress."

"It's probably better if you don't know," Mel said, which was her way of stalling for an answer because she really had no idea what she was going to do with it.

"You're right." Joyce gave her one more solid hug and then stood waving while Mel pulled away.

If the dress had to be destroyed, she supposed she could bag it and put it in a Dumpster. But then someone might fish it out and resurrect it and, with her luck, Joyce would run into that person at the library or the post office. South Scottsdale was like that.

She debated chopping it up and make a pair of bright blue pillows out of it. Nah, her mom would freak if she saw them in Mel's apartment. The dress had to die, but how?

She spun her Mini Cooper back towards Old Town and zipped along Camelback Road until she was just south of Tate's penthouse apartment. Ding! He had an outdoor gas grill. That would work.

Tate owned one of four corner penthouses in a luxury building that sat on the north side of the canal. She parked in the garage below his building and called him to make sure he was home. Then she zipped up to the top floor, clutching the Dillard's bag.

When the elevator announced her arrival, the doors slid open to reveal a marble foyer, tastefully decorated with large topiary bushes and long mirrors. Tate was standing in the open door of his penthouse, looking as if he'd been about to go to bed.

" 'Of all the gin joints in all the towns in all the world, she walks into mine,' " Tate said, doing a very bad Humphrey Bogart impression.

"Casablanca," Mel said, identifying the quote. "Way too easy."

"I know, but I just caught the end of it on the big screen, and now it's stuck in my head. He never should have let her get on that plane."

"Agreed."

"So, what brings you here?" Tate asked.

"I need a favor," she said. "I have to burn my mom's dress."

"What did it do to you?" He ushered her into the apartment.

"Not me — her. She's convinced it's cursed."

"That's . . ."

"Crazy?" Mel supplied.

"I was going to say highly imaginative."

They paused in the kitchen, where Mel stopped to get a glass of water.

"So, can I fire up your gas grill?" she asked.

"Have at it," he said. "That thing burns so hot it's almost an incinerator."

"I know. Remember those steaks we cooked when you first got it?"

"You mean the charcoal we made? Yeah, I remember. It took weeks for my eyebrows to grow back."

They stepped through one of the open glass doors that led to the veranda. More topiary plants, trimmed into the shape of flying birds, decorated the marble balcony. The view of downtown Scottsdale was all plush dark sky and twinkling lights, with the city of Phoenix visible beyond in another layer of lights. Mel felt a peace settle over her as she looked down at the hustle and bustle of the streets below.

A soft breeze blew across the balcony, and she waited while Tate started up the grill and set it for optimum heat.

"Have you talked to Angie today?" she asked.

"No, I sent her a text earlier, but I haven't heard back. Why?"

Mel wondered what to say, if anything. Oh, who was she kidding? Angie had a date. This was news!

"She's probably busy," she said. "Shopping for her date and all."

"Her what?" Tate whipped around. "What did you say?"

"Her date. Angie has a date."

The thermometer on the grill was reaching its high point. Tate stared stupidly at her while Mel lifted up the lid on the steel grill. A blast of heat hit her face, and she felt as if it had singed her eyelashes. Quickly, she took her mother's dress out of the bag and tossed it on the grill.

There was a loud *whoosh* sound as the blue fabric ignited. A terrible smell filled the veranda, and Tate reached around her to slam the lid shut.

"Good grief, what is that thing made of, formaldehyde?"

They both gagged and stepped back from the grill.

"Hey, you don't think the police would find it odd that you just torched the dress your mother was wearing on the night she had a date with a man who was murdered, do you?"

Mel looked at the grill and back at Tate. "Now? You point that out to me now? Not before I toss it on the flames?"

"Sorry, I just thought of it," he said.

"Well, I'm sure they could make something of it, but that would be ridiculous. I mean, it's just a dress," Mel said. "Right?"

"I need a drink," Tate said and led the way to the other side of the veranda, which housed a wet bar with a mini-fridge. He reached in and grabbed two beers, Fat Tires, and handed one to Mel.

They were quiet for a while, watching a noxious dark gray smoke seep out from under the lid of the grill.

"Angie hasn't had a date in . . ." He paused.

"A long time."

Actually, it had been since Angie and Tate had flown to Paris to visit Mel while she was taking a course at a culinary school there. According to Angie, it had been a passionate flight over the pond in Tate's private jet, but Tate had stopped it from becoming a habitual thing for the sake of their friendship. Angie thought it was because he was in love with Mel, but Mel didn't agree. In twenty-two years of friendship, she had never gotten that feeling from Tate. Never. Not once.

No, Mel suspected that Tate was afraid that if he and Angie hooked up, then their triad of friendship would suffer. Given that it was the thing that had seen them through awkward adolescence and turbulent college years, and now maintained their stability in adulthood, well, she understood why he hesitated.

Mel had only discovered recently that Angie had been in love with Tate since they were kids. Mel had never guessed, would never have guessed, if it hadn't been for Tate's recent engagement. Angie had been beside herself, and Mel had finally figured out that it was because she was in love with Tate. But if Mel hadn't figured it out, then she couldn't be terribly surprised that Tate hadn't either. Angie was very good at hiding her feelings.

She watched Tate closely. How did he feel about Angie having a date? He looked pensive, but that could mean anything.

"Who's the guy?" he asked, taking a long sip from his beer.

"No one you know," Mel said. "He came into the shop today."

"A total stranger?" he asked. Pensive switched to alarmed. "She's going out with a stranger? Do the brothers know about this?"

Mel laughed. "I don't think she's going to tell them."

"What about Joe?" Tate asked. "Are you going to tell him?"

"I hadn't planned to," Mel said. "Since we're going on the date, I'm not that worried."

"We're going?"

"Yes, Angie scored us tickets to his show," Mel said.

"Show?" Tate raised an eyebrow.

"Are you ready for this?" Mel asked and Tate nodded. "Angie has a date with Roach from the Sewers."

Tate's jaw slid open. "You're kidding. I love those guys.

"Na na na. Na na na. Step on this! Yeah,

step on this! Like this? Yeah!"

He sang the lyrics just as badly as Angie, and Mel was suddenly grateful that Roach was not here to hear it.

"So, Roach came into the shop? That is so cool."

"Sort of," Mel said. "Do you know his real name?"

"It's *not* Roach? Really?" He lifted the bottle to his lips.

"No, it's Brian Malloy."

Tate lowered his beer. "No way."

"Way." Mel took a long sip of her beer. "And now he's got the hots for Ange, and we're all going to his show tomorrow night."

Tate looked confounded, but before Mel could say anything else, her phone chimed. She knew it had to be her mother looking for a status report.

She flipped open her phone. "Relax, Mom. I took care of it. The dress has been destroyed."

"Interesting," a man's voice said. "And why exactly did you feel the need to destroy a piece of evidence?"

Mel felt all of the blood drain from her face. She knew that voice. It was deep and growly and sounded like it was in a perpetual state of annoyance. It was Detective

Martinez from the Paradise Valley Police Department, and he did not sound happy.

EIGHT

"On a scale of one to ten, how mad are you?"

Silence was Joe's only response.

"Because it's really hard for me to tell with your jaw clamped shut like that."

It was late, and they were driving from Joyce's house to Mel's apartment. Detective Martinez had questioned Mel and her mother for two hours upon learning that Mel had burned her mother's dress. For some reason, he didn't believe her mother thought the dress was cursed, but instead thought they were trying to destroy evidence. He'd even sent a forensic unit over to Tate's to take samples from the grill.

The interrogation only ended because Uncle Stan and Joe arrived and went nose to nose with Detective Martinez. When the detective accused Joe of covering up for his girlfriend, Mel was sure Joe was going to slug him. The detective even grinned at him as if hoping Joe would lose his cool. Instead, Joe had turned to Mel and said, "Get your things. This interview is over."

Uncle Stan had muscled Detective Martinez out the door on their heels and slammed it in his face.

While Joe helped Mel into his car, she heard the detective call, "This isn't over, DeLaura."

"Oh, yes, it is," Joe muttered under his breath before he roared out of her mother's driveway.

"What were you thinking?" Joe finally spoke. "Do you have any idea how this looks?"

"Bad?" Mel guessed.

"Detective Martinez is now suspicious that your mother had something to do with Malloy's murder," he said. "They were looking at Malloy's son, but now . . ."

"Funny you should mention him. Brian, right? Yeah, well, Angie's got a date with him," Mel said. Joe whipped his head in her direction with an incredulous expression.

She wasn't proud of herself, but Mel knew that one way to stop Joe from being mad at her was to throw Angie under the wheels of the overprotective-big-brother bus. She felt a little bad about it, but she promised herself she'd make it up to Angie one day.

They turned into the parking lot behind the bakery, and Joe stomped on the brakes of his black Prius, making them screech.

"Explain," he demanded. He hit the button to lock the doors of the car, keeping Mel right where she was.

"Roach, aka Brian Malloy, came into the shop today because he thought I was the woman dating his father, and he thought I killed him for some nefarious reason of my own," she said. "Angie set him straight, and I think he was quite taken with her, because he asked her out, and she said yes."

"But he's . . ."

"A drummer in a rock band, who goes by the name Roach," Mel said.

"I was thinking he's a murder suspect, but the rock-band thing isn't winning me over either," he said.

"Quite a pickle, isn't it?" She reached over Joe and pushed the button to unlock the doors. "I'm guessing you want to go talk to her, so I won't keep you. Call me."

She shoved open her door and was halfway out when a strong hand grabbed the tail of her shirt and hauled her back into the car. She landed back in her seat with a thud.

"Why do I get the feeling that dating you is career suicide?" he asked. He didn't wait for an answer but kissed her with an incendiary heat that made Tate's grill seem like a Bunsen burner.

"Go," he said, releasing her with a rueful smile. "Flip the light on twice, so I know you're safe."

Mel scraped her limp body off the expensive leather seat and hurried up the staircase to her apartment above. She unlocked the door, peered inside the studio apartment, and flipped the light switch off and on so that Joe knew she was safe. She watched as he drove away and then collapsed onto her futon with an exhaustion she hadn't known was possible.

The first person in the door when the bakery opened the next morning was Mr. Zelaznik. He shuffled in and demanded a four-pack of cupcakes and a glass of water.

"Breakfast of champions," Angie said as she went to fill his order.

Mel had been watching Angie all morning. She hadn't said anything about Tate or Joe, so Mel was left to wonder if either of them had said anything to Angie about her date.

Just when she thought she couldn't take it anymore, Tate strolled in. He looked pensive — again.

"How did it go last night with the detectives?" he asked, taking a seat at the counter.

"It could have gone better," Mel said. She opened the back of the display case and began shifting cupcakes to make room for a fresh batch of Orange Dreamsicle Cupcakes. It was one of her favorites, an orange cupcake topped with vanilla buttercream and garnished with a candied orange peel.

"What detectives?" Angie asked as she came back from delivering Mr. Zelaznik's water.

Mel hadn't told Angie about the night before, because she didn't want to have to admit that she'd blabbed about Angie's date to save herself.

"It was no big deal," she said. "They just had some more questions."

"No big deal?" Tate gaped. "They impounded my grill."

"Come again?" Angie looked between the two of them as if they'd suddenly started speaking Swahili.

The bells on the door jangled, and in strode Roach, looking every inch the rock star that he was. Angie broke into a smile at the sight of him, and he grinned at her in return.

Hopping up and leaning over the counter, he planted a kiss on her that did not give Mel the impression that this was new territory for him.

"I missed you," he said, tossing his long black hair over his shoulder. "I have a few hours before rehearsal. Come away with me."

"I . . ." Angie glanced at Tate and Mel. "Um . . . we ran into each other at RA, the sushi restaurant, and . . ." Her voice trailed off, and her cheeks flushed bright pink.

"Ange, I don't think . . ." Tate began, but she froze him with a hard stare and said, "Let's keep it that way."

Angie glanced back at Roach. Then she took off her apron and tossed it onto Tate's shoulder. "You can cover for me, right partner?"

"But . . . but I . . ." Tate stammered.

"I'll meet you guys later for the show," she said. She tucked her hand around Roach's elbow, and with a wave he led her to the door. It shut behind them with a soft sigh, and Tate turned to Mel.

"She's dating that? Our Angie is dating that?"

"Tate, you knew it was Roach from the Sewers. He looks just like he does in his videos. What's the surprise?"

"How is it he knows her well enough to kiss her like that?"

"I guess they had a good time last night."

Mel shrugged.

"Last night?" Tate huffed. "Before I had a chance to check him out? He could be a murderer! Has she thought of that? Huh?"

"Oh, I wouldn't go there if I were you," Mel said. She still had scorch marks from Angie's temper yesterday when she'd forbidden her to date a possible murderer.

"Did you see those tattoos?" Tate continued. "They look like jailhouse tattoos to me."

"I thought he looked cool," Mr. Zelaznik said around a mouthful of cupcake. "I bet I could get any babe I wanted if I looked like him."

"Well, who asked you?" Tate snapped.

Mel tied the apron on Tate, ignoring his hysterics.

"Why don't you go get another batch of cupcakes from the cooler?" she suggested. "I think you need some time to chill."

Tate grunted and, still muttering, banged through the door to the kitchen.

Mel shook her head. It appeared Angie had finally gotten Tate's notice. But judging by how happy she looked with Roach, maybe it was too late.

Tate helped Mel load the cupcake display case. From his silence, she could tell he was still fuming about Angie and her date. She put him to work wiping down the tables before the post-lunch rush while she boxed up several special orders in back and put them in the cooler to await pickup.

Tate was just putting away his cleaning supplies in the closet when his phone rang its distinctive James Bond theme. He yanked it out of his pocket and checked it.

"Yes! I've been waiting for this," he said to Mel. "Do you mind if I take it in your office?"

"Not at all," she said.

She glanced at Mr. Zelaznik, who had looked up from his cupcakes and crossword, and they both shrugged.

While it was quiet, Mel decided to fold up some four-pack boxes. In addition to Mr. Zelaznik's three entries today, there had been five more entries in the Fairy Tale Cupcake contest this morning alone. Most surprising was the fact that they were men. Mel had a feeling that with Valentine's Day rapidly approaching, guys were looking for something special for their significant others, and wasn't a night on the town topped with cupcakes just perfect?

Maybe there would even be a run on four-packs of cupcakes. She was crouched down behind the counter to pull out a stack of flat boxes to be folded into four-pack carriers when she heard the door chime.

"I'll be right with you," she called.

"Where's Angie?"

"Is she in back?"

"We need to talk to her."

"Pronto."

Uh-oh. Mel stayed hunkered down behind the counter. The DeLaura brothers were here. It sounded like all seven of them. No, Joe would have called her if he was coming over. That meant the rest of them were here, and they were not going to be happy when they found out Angie wasn't.

Mel wondered if she could crawl out the kitchen door before they noticed her.

Tony, the tallest, leaned over the counter and spotted her. "Hi, Mel."

She sighed and slowly rose to her feet. Six of the seven DeLaura brothers stood before her: Dom, Ray, Sal, Tony, Paulie, and Al. Angie's brothers. It was a bit overwhelming to be confronting six good-looking variations of her boyfriend Joe. She couldn't help but notice that the level of testosterone in the bakery had risen to a level she'd never before experienced.

"Hi, boys. What brings you in today?"

"I do," Tate said from behind her. He was standing in the doorway and, even in his pink Fairy Tale Cupcakes apron, he looked

106

resolute. "Gentlemen, if you'll follow me."

"What are you, mob owned?" Mr. Zelaznik called to Mel from his table. "Is this just a cover operation for a house of ill repute?"

"No!" she snapped. "It most certainly is not."

"Darn," Mr. Zelaznik said as he stuffed in another bite of cupcake.

Mel pushed through the swinging doors after the last of the DeLaura brothers and stared at Tate as if he'd lost his mind. He met her stare, refusing to back down.

She grabbed him by the elbow and hauled him into the corner and hissed, "Did you call them all here? Does the term *dead man walking* mean anything to you?"

"What?" Tate asked. "Angie could be out there with a murderer right now. We need to strategize."

"Tate, she is going to murder *you* for dragging the brothers into this," Mel warned.

"If it means keeping her safe, I'll risk it," he said.

Melanie just shook her head. "I notice Joe isn't here."

"Yeah, he seemed to think you and Angie would not be on board with this plan."

"You think?"

"Hey, Mel, how about a round of cupcakes?" Paulie asked.

"My treat," Tate said and Mel turned to glower at him.

"You got that right," she said.

She pushed through the swinging doors and loaded up a tray with a half dozen cupcakes and glasses of milk, except for one glass of iced tea for Sal, because he was lactose intolerant.

When she reentered the kitchen, Tate was pacing in front of the brothers, who were all seated on stools around the steel worktable, watching him with varying levels of concern.

"This Roach character," Dom said. "How long has she known him? And what kind of name is that anyway?"

"It's his stage name, and they met yester-day, right Mel?" Tate asked.

"Oh, no. I am not a party to this," Mel said.

"But he could be a murderer!" Tate said. "And she's your best friend. How can you be so unconcerned?"

"I'm concerned, but I also trust Angie's judgment," Mel said. "Besides, he has no reason to harm her. I saw the way he looked at her this morning. I think he really likes her."

"How did he look at her?" Ray asked. He dropped his fork and cracked his knuckles.

"Like he wanted to see her naked," Tate said.

Several hands slammed down on the steel worktable, and the brothers growled. It sounded as if Mel had a bear trapped in her kitchen. She raised her hands in frustration.

"Stop it!" she ordered. "Just stop it. Do any of you know why Angie has been single for the better part of the past fifteen years?"

"No one's good enough for our Ange," Sal said. "It would take a very special guy to deserve someone like her, and she hasn't found him yet."

"Yeah," Al agreed. He was the only De-Laura who still lived at home, and Mel had a soft spot for him because he was the one who most resembled Joe.

"No, it's because you thugs chase away every single man she's interested in," Mel said. "And if you do it again, I'm afraid you're going to lose her."

"What do you mean lose her?" Tony asked. He shoved in the last of his cupcake and swallowed.

"I mean that Roach is a rock musician who lives in Los Angeles and goes on tour quite a bit. If you try to mess this up for Angie, she may leave to go on the road with him," Mel said.

"Nah, this is Angie we're talking about,"

Paulie said. "She could never leave her family."

"Don't be so sure," Mel said. She glanced at Tate, who looked as determined as a bulldog tracking a bone, and she felt like whacking him on the head with her tray. She resisted the urge — barely.

"Mel, remember that I told you I was going to check out Baxter's business? Well, I've gotten some disturbing information," Tate said. "Which is why I think Angie needs to stay as far as possible from anyone connected with Malloy, especially his son."

"What kind of information?"

"Baxter? That's the dead guy your mom went out with, isn't it?" Tony asked.

"Yes," Mel said. "Oh, and please thank your mom for the lasagna she sent over after the . . . uh . . . incident. It was very thoughtful of her."

"Will do," Al said.

"Baxter Malloy — or Bastard Malloy, as some of his former business associates call him — was operating a Ponzi scheme."

"A whatie scheme?" Ray asked.

"Ponzi," Sal answered. "It's when you offer fast, high returns to investors, but it's based on nothing but getting them to invest even more, so you're always paying them with their own money. Eventually it implodes,

and the more people who have invested, the more spectacular the losses."

"Exactly," Tate said. "Well, Malloy had hooked in some big money. In fact, my people at Harper Investments tell me he bilked billions out of unsuspecting investors."

"I don't see what this has to do with his son," Mel said. "Roach told us he hasn't spoken to his father in three years."

"Really?" Tate asked. "Because according to the partial list of investors I managed to obtain, Roach invested millions with his father and by all accounts has lost it all. I ran a credit check on him. He's broke."

"Well, that would give a guy a heck of a motive to off his own father," Dom said. "Especially if they weren't close to begin with."

"My thoughts exactly," Tate said. "Now Mel and I will be on Angie's date with her tonight, but we'll need you all to make sure she's not alone with him after that."

"Not a problem," Ray said. "We can take turns running interference."

The brothers spent the next half hour working out the shifts they planned to take to keep an eye on their sister. Mel tried to argue on Angie's behalf, but her effort was halfhearted. Honestly, now that Roach looked like such a promising suspect, she didn't like the idea of Angie dating him at all.

Finally, the DeLaura brothers trooped out. Mel and Tate followed them back into the main room, where Mr. Zelaznik was still sitting.

"You do realize what will happen if Angie finds out?" Mel asked.

"I'll deal with that if that happens," he said.

Mel didn't have the heart to tell him that it *would* happen, no doubt about that. She just hoped that Roach was more of a fling than the real thing for Angie; otherwise, she didn't think Angie would ever be able to forgive Tate.

"Mel, there's more," Tate said.

Something in his voice caused her to go still.

"Spill it," she said.

"Malloy's list of investors," he said. "Your mother's name is on that list, too."

NINE

"What?" Mel asked. She was certain she must have heard wrong.

"The detectives will be getting the same list, if they don't have it already," Tate said. "You can be sure they're going to ask your mother questions."

"Like what?" Mel asked. "She didn't know him. They'd just met. If she'd invested with him, I'm sure it was through a third party."

"I don't think the police are going to care how her money ended up in Baxter's care."

"Oh my God, this is a nightmare."

"On the upside," Tate began, but Mel interrupted.

"What upside?"

"From the peek I got, Malloy's investor list reads like the white pages for South Scottsdale. Virtually everyone who is anyone had something tied up with him."

"That should make my mother look innocent, right?"

"Except for the fact that she was barely dressed with his body floating in the pool, yeah," he said.

"Your mother got naked with that shyster?" Mr. Zelaznik called from his booth.

"Half naked," Mel snapped.

"Think she'd go out with me?" he asked. He looked as eager as a puppy; even his hair hat stood aquiver at the thought.

"No!" Mel and Tate said together. Mr. Zelaznik slumped down in his seat.

"We need to find out who had the most invested with him," Mel said. "But how?"

"That's easy," Tate said. "They're all attending the annual fundraiser luncheon at the Scottsdale Museum of Contemporary Art."

"How do you know this?" Mel asked.

Tate pulled an invitation out of his pocket and said, "Because anyone who is anyone in South Scottsdale was invited."

"Harper Investments has a table," she said.

"Naturally. So, shall I squeeze you in?"

Mel took the invitation. Scanning the back, she read the list of restaurants contributing to the event. Dessert was being provided by Confections, featuring cupcakes. Surprise, surprise; the giant cupcake, Olivia Puckett, had wormed her way into the charity event.

Mel thought about it for a moment.

"Sorry, Tate, you're not going to the luncheon."

"What do you mean?"

"You're going to be too busy keeping Olivia from delivering her dessert to attend."

"I'm going to what?"

"You heard me," Mel said. "But I'm going to need another body."

She tapped the invitation against her chin. If only Angie were here, she could get her to help. Oh, well, she was out of options.

"Mr. Zelaznik, how would you like to earn three free raffle entries for the Fairy Tale Cupcake contest?"

He looked warily at her. "Depends on what I have to do. You don't want me to whack anybody, do you?"

"No! Do you own black pants and a white shirt?" she asked.

"Yeah." Still, he looked suspicious.

"Can you pose as a waiter?" she asked.

He lifted a scrawny old-man arm and patted his bicep. "I think I can manage it for ten free entries."

"Five," Mel countered.

"Seven," he haggled.

"Done," Mel agreed. "Let's get to work,

115

fellas. We're going to crash a party."

" 'Either I'm off my nut, or he is . . . or you are!' " Tate said an hour later while they stuffed Mel's Mini Cooper with boxes of cupcakes.

"George Bailey in *It's a Wonderful Life,*" Mel said, citing the quote. "And I'm not off my nut. People talk more freely around the hired help. It's a fact."

"How do you think you're just going to waltz into a luncheon and pass yourself off as Olivia Puckett?"

"Puleeeeze. I've done this catering shtick a million times. I know the drill."

Tate didn't look convinced.

For his part, Mr. Zelaznik looked more than game. In his crisp white shirt and snappy black bow tie, he carried himself with a certain dapperness that had been missing beneath his well-worn cardigan. Mel debated making him lose the hair hat, but it was sort of growing on her; besides, she didn't have time to argue if he kicked up a fuss.

He and Mel drove to the museum in her car while Tate headed out to stall Olivia. His grand plan so far was to double park behind her big, pink refrigerator van so that she couldn't leave to get to the luncheon.

116

Mel pulled into the loading dock next to two other catering trucks. Waitstaff dressed in the standard white shirts and black pants were buzzing from the vans to the back door as they unloaded the day's luncheon.

Mel found the event coordinator in the kitchen and introduced herself.

"I'm here with dessert," she said, intentionally vague.

The woman, whose name tag read Bonnie, checked her clipboard. "I don't see . . . oh, wait. Cupcakes. Yes, here you are. You're early. Dessert won't be served for another hour."

"No problem," Mel said. "We'll just store our cupcakes in the cooler and pitch in until it's time."

"Fine. If you need anything, let me know," Bonnie said. Her hair was up in a French twist, and her chic purple wraparound dress hugged a nice set of curves that made her look feminine without appearing too easy-access.

She and Mr. Zelaznik made quick work of unloading the cupcakes into the walk-in refrigerator in the kitchen. The executive chef and Bonnie seemed to be having a disagreement about the temperature of the cold soups, and Mel was more than happy to leave the kitchen before it turned ugly.

"Okay, Mr. Zelaznik," she began, but he interrupted.

"Call me Marty, since I'm staff now and all."

Mel smiled. "All right, Marty. I want you to work the room. Blend in as much as you can, and keep your ears open for any talk about Baxter Malloy."

"Will do," he agreed.

"Report back to me in the kitchen in forty-five minutes," Mel said. She watched as he shuffled off in the direction of a cluster of ladies. *Go, Marty, go!*

Meanwhile, she headed in the opposite direction: into the museum. As soon as she stepped through the door, she paused to check out the crowd. It was made up of the same people who always made up these events. You had your Generation O, as in *old.* These were the folks who still wore cowboy hats and chunky turquoise jewelry, who had been residents of the city since the 1950s, when Frank Sinatra used to sing for his supper at the Safari and when the introduction of air conditioning made Arizona more habitable.

Then you had your younger, more newly minted money, usually discernable by the amount of cleavage and leg being shown, although some of the older ladies were giving healthy glimpses of their gams, too. Zapping those pesky spider veins with lasers will do that for a gal, or so Mel had heard.

The men all looked the same: Old or new money, they sported potbellies and receding hairlines, thin gold watches, and citrus-scented cologne. Conversation revolved around golf handicaps, exotic cruises recently taken, and how much money they had spent on luxury cars for their wives.

The women ran the gamut of shapes and sizes. The only things they all seemed to have in common were expensive clothing, expensive hairdos, gobs of jewelry, and a withering disdain for the husbands who provided it all.

Mel grabbed an empty tray from a side table. She wandered through the room gathering empty glasses, keeping her head down and her ears open. She saw two women whispering together and leaned in close.

"She's had more work than Joan Rivers."

"Botox?"

"Collagen, an acid peel, and a full lift. Look, her eyebrows practically reach her hairline."

Mel glanced up to see who they were whispering about. In a too-tight micro-minidress, she was easy to spot. Under a huge blonde weave, the woman's face looked as if it were molded from plastic. When she spoke, her face didn't even move. Creepy. Mel shuddered.

The guests were ushered into one of the larger galleries where banquet tables had been set up. Mel deposited her tray in the kitchen and grabbed a water pitcher, heading back out to the banquet room to fill up glasses as the guests seated themselves.

"I heard Malloy was bludgeoned to death with a Marc Jacobs stiletto."

Bingo!

Mel circled back to stand near a gossipy gathering of women. The one speaking was one of the Generation Os. She was stout, dressed in clothes designed to hide extra pounds, her fingers sparkled with many rings, and her short hair was dyed the color of champagne. Her voice was hushed as she repeated her gossip, but it also carried a note of macabre delight.

"You would be wrong, Doreen," said another woman. She was also of the older set. She was rail thin and her silver hair was cut in a stylish bob. She wore a Dolce & Gabbana floral dress with black trim, which set off a stunning onyx necklace with matching drop earrings and a large ring on her right hand.

She adjusted her napkin in her lap with

the air of one who is used to commanding attention. The nine ladies dining with her all leaned forward, and one of the younger-looking ones whispered, "Oh, Beverly, what have you heard?"

Mel found herself leaning in as well. A dribble of ice water ran over her hand, and she jerked herself back, remembering that she was supposed to be a waitress. She snatched up a glass and began to fill it while the woman named Beverly spoke.

"Well, he was not bludgeoned, he was strangled."

"I bet it was that slut he was on a date with," one of the women said.

Mel bristled on her mother's behalf and turned to glare at the woman. She was a buxom blonde, pushing fifty but trying to hold on to thirty-five with a clenched fist.

Mel's eyes narrowed. She knew this woman. She was the one Joyce had snapped at in the dressing room at Dillard's.

"I actually saw her the day before the date," the woman said.

"You didn't!" another woman gasped.

"I did," the woman said. She looked smugly pleased to have the attention of the entire table. "Her name is something pedestrian. Joy . . . er, no. Joyce. That's it. I imagine she has oodles of money, otherwise

I can't imagine what Baxter saw in such a frumpy little woman."

Mel wanted to dump the entire pitcher of ice water into the shrew's lap, but the older lady named Beverly in the onyx jewels lifted her water glass, and Mel had no choice but to fill it or blow her cover.

Beverly frowned at the blonde. It was obvious from her pinched expression that she did not like sharing the limelight.

She turned her head towards the blonde, raised a slim, penciled-on eyebrow, and asked, "Correct me if I'm wrong, but weren't you dating Baxter, Elle?"

Mel glanced back at Elle, the blonde, who pouted and said, "A few times. Hardly worth mentioning."

"Really? Didn't he buy you that lovely pink solitaire?" Beverly asked.

Elle lowered her right hand under the table, but not before Mel caught a flash of pink. Beverly looked like a shark that smelled blood in the water and was circling back for the killing strike. "In fact, didn't Baxter pay for your townhouse and your Cadillac? One wonders, how are you going to maintain them now?"

The blonde flushed a sickly shade of red, and Mel knew it was no coincidence that she had been in the dressing room that day.

She must have been following them in order to check Joyce out, no doubt to see who her competition was.

"Seems to me the police should be asking you some questions about Baxter's death, especially if he was, oh, how shall I put it — moving on?"

"Trading up," said another, and they all cackled.

Elle rose to her feet and tossed her napkin onto the table.

"Enjoy yourself now, Beverly. Your days of being among the elite are numbered."

"Oh, am I to be replaced by you?" Beverly asked. Her eyes flashed angrily, and Mel got the distinct impression that there was a history between these two women and that this was more than just a power play among women.

"You've already had one heart attack. I don't suppose you'll survive another. More butter?" Elle picked up a small crock of butter and smacked it down on the table in front of Beverly. "Eat up."

She whirled around, her hot pink Alexander McQueen dress flashing like a strobe light as she strode out of the room with a fury that spewed behind her like exhaust fumes.

"I never liked her," the woman named

Doreen said. "She's just trash. I can't believe she thinks she can get away with talking to you like that."

Mel glanced at Beverly, who seemed completely unaffected by Elle's outburst. In fact, she wore a small smile of satisfaction.

She glanced around the table at the ladies and said, "Oh, she won't get away with it. Do you see that tall gentleman by the door? He's a police officer."

The women all turned to stare. Mel did, too, and her breath tripped on her inhale and left her gasping. Leaning against the wall watching their group was Detective Martinez. She could hear the blood rushing through her ears and felt her face get hot. Had he seen her? How would she explain?

As she watched, he turned and followed Elle as she stomped out the door to the museum. Mel went limp with relief.

"Do you really think it was Elle who killed Malloy?" one of the women squeaked. She had pointy features and short hair dyed a startling shade of red. She leaned close to the other women as if nervous.

"She had an awful lot to lose if he dumped her," one woman said.

"I heard the police found his date buck naked and drunk in the Jacuzzi while he was dead in the pool," said another.

"No!" gasped another woman. Now Mel had to curb the urge to dump the ice water on the lot of them.

"So, who was she? This Joy . . . er, Joyce person?"

"A gold digger, no doubt," Beverly said. "You know the type, all blonde and tan and surgically enhanced. Probably just a younger version of Elle."

Mel glanced around the table. Six of the nine remaining ladies definitely fit that description, and yet they nodded in accord with Beverly. Mel had to wonder: When a person became a stereotype, did they really not know it?

"What will happen to Malloy's company?" one of the blondes asked.

"Will it go to his son?" another asked.

"Oh, I should hope not," Beverly said. "He's a disgrace. All those years at Juilliard, and he plays in a rock-and-roll band." She sniffed in disgust.

The woman's contempt made Mel feel warmer towards Roach, even though he was possibly a murderer and currently out with her best friend, than she would have if Beverly had approved of him.

"Oh, look, there's Jay Gatwick," the pointy-featured woman said. All eyes turned towards a table across the room.

"How did Poppy manage to bag him?"

"I heard that they met on the Ponte Vecchio in Firenze," Doreen said. "He took one look at her and knew he had to marry her."

A collective sigh went around the table, emitted by every woman except Beverly. She was looking at the Gatwicks with a contemplative stare.

"He is divine, isn't he?" one woman asked.

"I don't know," Beverly said. "You know the old expression. If something seems to be too good to be true, it usually is."

"Now, Beverly, just because he isn't your Morty doesn't mean he isn't a fine man," Doreen said.

A flash of pain crossed over Beverly's face, and Mel recognized it for what it was. Grief. She'd seen the same anguished look on her mother's face. So Beverly was a widow, then. Mel decided to forgive her for her uncharitable comments about her mother. She couldn't help but feel empathy for anyone who had lost her spouse.

"No, he isn't Morty," Beverly said. "No one is."

Mel glanced back over at the Gatwicks. Even though they were students in her cupcake class, she supposed it would be bad form to go over and say hello, seeing as she was posing as the hired help under false pretenses and all.

As the table went on to discuss the Gatwicks and the latest party Jay had thrown in honor of Poppy, Mel figured the good gossip was over and it was time to get back to the kitchen.

As she wound her way through the crowd, she tried to keep an eye out for Detective Martinez on the off chance he reappeared and recognized her. Hopefully he wasn't looking too closely at the waitstaff.

She was halfway through the room when she felt a tap on her shoulder.

"Hello, Melanie." It was Jay Gatwick. "What brings you here?"

"Dessert," Mel said, gesturing at her white shirt and black pants.

"Oh, I didn't realize you were catering," he said. "I thought it was some other bakery. Poppy's on the board, you know, and recommended you, but apparently the baker they had in mind has been doing it for years. Poppy got the distinct impression that the other board members were afraid of her."

"Er, something must have happened. I was a last minute fill-in," Mel said. It wasn't a complete lie, she told herself.

"Well, aren't we the lucky ones? We get to enjoy the ambrosia of your ovens." That was the charm of Jay Gatwick. He could say the dopiest things and not sound at all like a dork. Very Cary Grant.

"Thanks," Mel said.

"I owe you an apology, by the way," he said.

"You do?"

"Yes, the other night at class, when you asked me if I'd heard of Baxter Malloy . . . well, I guess we've all heard of him now."

"Yes," Mel agreed with a heavy sigh.

"Poppy and I were wondering . . ." Jay paused as if uncertain of how to continue.

Mel decided to save him the trouble. "Yes, it was my mother he was with when he was found dead."

"Oh." Jay looked away. "I'm sorry. That must have been awful for her."

"She was shaken up, but she'll be all right," Mel said. "She's survived worse. I'm just afraid the police have fixated on her because she actually had money invested with Malloy and didn't even know it."

Jay gave her a hard look, and then in a hushed voice he said, "That describes most of this room."

"What do you know?" Mel asked.

Jay took her elbow and steered her towards the wall.

"Look over my left shoulder," he said.

"See the man in the gray suit at table twelve."

"The one with the *Magnum P.I.* mustache?" she asked.

Jay smiled. "Scottie Jensen, played for the Dodgers, headed for the hall of fame. Lost everything. I heard they foreclosed on his house yesterday."

"That's terrible," Mel said.

"Check out table twenty," Jay said. "See the old couple in matching sweaters?"

"His and hers Norwegian knits?"

"That's Lester and Miriam Hargrave. Malloy wiped them out of billions."

"Billions?" Mel squeaked.

"Probably, all they can afford are the sweaters," Jay said with a shake of his head.

"What about that blonde who just stormed from the room?" Mel asked. "I heard she was dating Malloy."

"Elle Simpson," Jay said. "She's got a string of sugar daddies behind her, of which Malloy was the latest. Frankly, I'm surprised she hasn't been strangled by one of the women here."

Mel raised her eyebrows. "Do tell."

Jay tipped his head in the direction of the table Mel had just left. "Beverly Logan, queen of the socialites, would love to see Elle swing for Malloy's murder. Apparently,

Elle had a torrid affair with Beverly's beloved Morty just before he died."

"So that explains the tension between those two," Mel said. "Wow."

"What I'm saying is, don't worry about your mother. She'll be cleared. There were too many people with real motives."

"Thanks, Jay," Mel said. He made her feel better. "Hey, if you hear anything else, would you let me know?"

"You mean if I hear something suspicious?" he asked with a wiggle of his eyebrows.

"Yes, if someone happens to mention over the shrimp cocktail that they strangled Malloy in a fit of pique, that would be fabulous," she said.

He gave her a dazzling grin. "My ears are at your service."

"Excuse me, shouldn't you be in the kitchen?" Bonnie, the event coordinator, approached Mel with her clipboard. "Dessert is coming up fast. You need to be plating your cupcakes."

"Oh, yeah," Mel said. She gave Jay a small smile. "Duty calls."

Marty met her in the kitchen. Under the hustle and bustle of kitchen noise, he told her what he'd heard. The rumors of Malloy's murder were even wilder and included

Malloy being eviscerated by a broken martini glass. Mel could only assume the wealthy really enjoyed the drama of a grisly murder in their midst.

He, too, had heard that Elle was Malloy's lover and that she was angry that Malloy had been dating someone else. He'd also heard that the Hargraves and Scottie Jensen, along with others who'd lost money to Malloy's investment company, were under police scrutiny. Still, the consensus of the room was that Baxter had been offed by his date.

Using large circular trays, Mel quickly plated her cupcakes onto dessert plates, putting pink cocktail napkins stamped with the Fairy Tale Cupcakes logo under each cupcake. She used these when she catered and, even if she had muscled Olivia out of this gig, she wasn't about to let the other baker take credit for her cupcakes.

There was a wide variety of flavors, from Death by Chocolate to Tinkerbells, so the guests wouldn't have to fight it out for the flavors they wanted.

She shouldered a tray and headed towards the swinging doors when the cell phone in her pocket went off. She put the tray back down and went to shut her phone off. It would be bad form to serve with her *Gone with the Wind* ringtone blaring out of her pocket.

She glanced at the display and saw that it was Tate. Uh-oh.

"Tate, what's up?"

"The baker is on the move," he said. His voice was high-pitched and a little hysterical.

"What?" Mel asked.

"The baker is on the move," he said. "I double-parked just like I planned, and she had me towed. Can you freaking believe that?"

Yeah, that actually seemed reasonable to Mel.

"What's her ETA?" Mel asked.

"Ten minutes if she hits all the lights right," he said.

Mel shut her phone. "Marty, we've got ten minutes. Move it."

Mel and Marty hit the doors with their trays up high as if someone had lit their backsides on fire. Mel grabbed two waiters who were standing idly by and drafted them into helping. In minutes, every table was served.

Mel didn't even take the time to feel gratified by the *ooh*s and *aah*s her cupcakes received. Instead, she grabbed Marty and bolted for the door.

132

"Let's go, let's go," she yelled.

Mel ran as fast as she could while dragging a seventy-something-year-old man behind her. Bonnie stood gaping as they passed her, obviously losing her powers of speech at the spectacle they created.

They almost made it, too.

TEN

Mel hit the back door just as a pink refrigerator van screeched into the lot.

"You!" Olivia jumped out. Her cheeks were flushed, and her corkscrew gray hair was wild on top of her head. Her nostrils flared, and Mel waited for her to paw at the ground with one of her rubber-soled shoes.

"Marty, walk backwards really slowly into the kitchen," Mel instructed. He shuffled back, and Mel followed, never taking her eyes off of Olivia.

As if sensing her prey was about to escape, Olivia charged, shouting, "I know what you're up to Melanie Cooper, and it won't work!"

Mel skirted around Marty, grabbed him by the hand, and, pulling him behind her, dashed into the dining room, thinking there was no way Olivia would interrupt the guests while they were eating. She was so wrong.

They hustled around Bonnie to the bar.

"Drink?" Marty asked. "A bourbon neat sure would hit the spot."

"Get down!" Mel said and yanked him down beside her.

The bartender gave them an alarmed look, but Mel put her fingers over her lips in a silent *shh.*

"I know you're in here!" Olivia shouted, and the entire dining room went silent. Mel imagined all seven hundred guests had turned to stare at Olivia.

Mel could feel her heart thumping against her rib cage. How was she going to get out of this?

"Stop, stop eating those cupcakes right now!" Olivia commanded in a voice tinged with hysteria. Indignant mutters broke out across the room. "You're supposed to be eating my cupcakes. Mine!"

Mel couldn't see what was going on, but it sounded like a ruckus had broken out. She glanced up from her crouched position at the bartender's face. His eyes were wide, and his mouth had slid open and stayed agape.

"Give me that!" Olivia demanded.

"Get your hands off my cupcake!" Mel recognized the voice as belonging to Beverly.

"You're not supposed to eat that!" Olivia

snapped. "You're supposed to be eating mine."

"I don't want yours," Beverly said. "I like this one. The cake is moist, the frosting-to-cake ratio is perfect, and the buttercream, well, it's positively divine. The best I've ever tasted."

Mel flushed with pleasure and almost popped up from behind the bar to receive her due. Marty shook his head at her, and she sank back down.

"Ouch!" Olivia howled.

"What happened?" Mel asked the bartender.

"The crazy lady tried to take the other woman's cupcake, and the other woman jabbed the crazy lady with her fork!" he said.

"I'm going to have to ask you to leave now, Ms. Puckett," Bonnie demanded.

"You can't kick me out! I'm listed on the invitation. Confections is providing dessert," Olivia protested.

"As you can see, dessert has already been taken care of," Bonnie said. "And a good thing, too, since you were late."

"It wasn't my fault," Olivia protested. "Someone was double-parked — Wait a minute."

Mel could almost hear the thoughts click into place in Olivia's brain.

"Ms. Puckett, if you don't leave at once, I'm going to call security," Bonnie said. "This is not the time or place for this discussion."

Mel glanced up and saw the bartender looking scared. That could only mean one thing. Olivia was coming.

"Excuse me." He stepped over Mel and Marty and ducked out from behind the bar.

Mel glanced all around her to see if there was a weapon of any kind, because she fully expected Olivia to tear her limb from limb for this. A bucket of pop on ice was the only thing available, so she grabbed a can and shook it as hard as she could.

"Aha!" When Olivia's big head appeared over the bar, Mel popped the top and let the contents fly. Olivia sputtered and staggered back.

Mel dropped the can, yanked Marty to his feet, and dashed for the kitchen. The door was clear. They were going to make it, but Mel was moving too fast, and she didn't see it: one tiny little pat of butter. She stepped on it, and her shoe went out from under her. To his credit, Marty tried to catch her, but he had to sidestep Olivia, who was hot on their heels. Mel landed on the hard floor with a *smack,* and Olivia tripped over her and went careening into a collection of pots and pans that echoed with a horrific crash.

Mel scrambled to her knees and scooted for the back door, which Marty was very gallantly holding open.

A pair of sturdy black pumps blocked her exit. She slowly glanced up to find herself nose to knee with Bonnie. Her blonde twist had become unraveled, and her face was mottled in shades of red, which clashed with her purple dress.

"Get out!" she snapped.

"On my way," Mel said, and she continued scooting towards the door.

Behind her she heard Olivia moan, and over that she heard Bonnie tell Olivia that she was never, not under any circumstances, *ever* to volunteer her services for the annual arts drive again.

Once outside, Mel found that, in an ironic twist of karmic payback, Olivia's pink van was blocking her Mini Cooper. She heard Olivia shout her name, and she and Marty exchanged wide-eyed glances.

Mel spotted a Dumpster in the corner. Marty was too old to outrun Olivia; they were going to have to hide. She grabbed him by the elbow again and shoved him up against the side of the Dumpster.

"Hey, hey, hey," he protested. "I'm not

going in there."

"It's either that, or Olivia catches you," Mel said.

Marty scooted up the side with renewed vigor, and Mel jumped in after him. Her left hand landed in slimy raw eggs, and her right foot connected with a hollow melon rind. It was like playing Twister in hell.

She could hear Marty gagging from the stench, and she could feel her own breakfast surge up her esophagus, but she forced it back down as she heard the back door to the kitchen slam open.

"Mouth breathe," Mel instructed. "She's looking for us."

Marty made an audible swallow and was silent. They listened as Olivia stomped around the loading dock. She yelled at a busboy having a smoke and at an assistant chef, demanding to know where Mel and Marty had gone.

Mel prayed hard that no one had seen them. Finally, she heard Olivia's pink van start up and drive away.

She and Marty disentangled themselves from the piles of cold pasta, sour milk, and fish heads. Gingerly, they climbed out of the Dumpster and stood staring at each other. Marty had lost his hair hat and his bald dome gleamed in the afternoon sun.

Even covered in Dumpster ick, he looked better without the hair. Mel figured she'd tell him later.

A silver Lexus skidded into the lot, and Tate jumped out.

"I thought she'd never leave," he said. Abruptly, his face turned a shade of pea green, and he pinched his nose. "I smell vomit. Gross!"

"Actually, you smell Dumpster," Mel said. "Marty, can I give you a lift home?"

He nodded as he flicked julienned carrots off his shirt front.

"Better ride with the windows down," Tate said as he backed away. "I'll go man the bakery until you get back."

"Thanks," Mel said. She and Marty climbed into her car. As her eyes watered from their collective stench, she figured she'd have to get the car detailed, or the stink might become a permanent part of her upholstery.

They pulled up in front of the senior center where Marty lived. It was beautifully landscaped with a large fountain and a planter overflowing with yellow and red lantana. Mel saw a hummingbird pop up from the flowers nearby and zip away. She wondered if it could smell them. Great. Now they were even offending nature.

"That's her!" Marty said, and he clapped his hands to his head in a reflexive gesture. "Hey, my hair. Where's my hair?"

"I'm guessing you left it back in the Dumpster," Mel said.

"And you didn't say anything?" His eyes were wide with panic. "She can't see me like this."

He crouched down below the dashboard, and Mel looked out the windshield to see the woman who had him in such a state.

She was young, black-haired, and beautiful. Her olive skin glowed underneath her workout clothes, which showed healthy curves and some serious muscle. She had a bag slung over her shoulder and was making her way towards them.

"Don't let her see me," Marty pleaded.

"Oh, for Pete's sake." Mel grabbed a newspaper from the backseat and draped it over him.

The woman was just passing the car when she stopped and her nose wrinkled in disgust. She looked around her as if trying to find the origin of the odor. She even checked the bottoms of her shoes.

She was older than she had first appeared. Mel would have placed her in her late forties, so not a spring chicken, unless you were the dirty old man hunched next to her.

141

The woman moved on quickly without ever spotting Mel in the car, as if trying to outrun the smell. Once she had left in her own sedan, Marty popped up.

"You could tell a fella when he loses his hair, you know," he complained.

"You look better without it," Mel said. "Honestly, the hair wasn't doing a thing for you."

He didn't look like he believed her. "I'm never going to get Beatriz to date me now."

"How do you know her?" Mel asked. "She's too young to live here."

"She's my yoga instructor," he said.

"You take yoga?"

"What? A man can't take yoga?"

"No, it's not that," Mel said. "It's just — Don't you think she's a bit young for you?"

Marty opened the door and swung his feet out. He looked back over his shoulder at Mel. "All my life I was a good and dutiful husband and father. I worked hard and provided well and loved them with all that I had. Then the kids grew up and moved away, and Jeanie died."

His words slowed, and he said, "There didn't seem to be much reason to get up anymore — and then I saw her. I've never dated a beautiful woman. You know, the sort of woman who can stop people in their tracks and make them forget what they're doing? So, if not now, when?"

He shut the door gently behind him, and Mel watched as he gingerly walked towards the entrance of the building. A piece of linguine stuck out of the back of his pants, and a tomato slice dragged off the back of his right heel.

If not now, when indeed?

ELEVEN

Mel arrived back at Fairy Tale Cupcakes. Her eyes had stopped watering, and her nose was plugged up with snot, obviously a self-defense mechanism. She didn't stop in the bakery, but hurried up the back stairs to her apartment to scour the ick off in her shower.

It took three lathers with soap and shampoo to get the stink out, but she finally managed it. Her stacked washer was already churning away at her clothes, but she figured she might have to run them through twice just to be sure.

Her short blonde hair dried quickly and, after pulling on fresh jeans and a sweater, she slipped on her sneakers and dashed down the stairs and into the kitchen.

She pushed through the back door, calling, "Tate!" but was startled by the sound of two men yelling and holding up her industrial-size cupcake tins as if they were shields.

"Ah!" She jumped back just as Tate came into the kitchen from the front. "Angie?"

"No, it's Mel," she said. The other two men lowered their cupcake pans, and Mel bit her lip to keep from laughing out loud.

"Um, Sal, is there any particular reason you are covered in blue paint splotches?" she asked Angie's older brother.

He glowered. She glanced at the other man. "You, too, Tony?"

He shrugged and went back to eating the vanilla cupcake on the table in front of him.

"She ambushed us," Sal explained.

"Angie?" Mel guessed.

"She lured us into an alley, and then she splattered us with a paintball gun," Tony said. "Tactically speaking, it was brilliant."

"Hunh," Sal grunted. He bit into his own cupcake and chewed. When he swallowed, he said, "Tate, has there been any word from unit B-2 or B-3?"

"None yet," Tate said. "I'm getting worried. They should have checked in by now."

"Tate, what exactly is going on?" Mel asked. "Who are B-2 and B-3?"

"Nothing's going on," he said, but his voice went up a notch, and she knew he was lying. "We're just doing a little Angie recon.

B-2 and B-3 stand for Brothers 2 and Brothers 3."

"Angie recon?" Mel repeated.

"Yeah, you know, making sure she's okay with that musician guy," he said.

"She is going to mur —"

Whatever Mel was about to say was cut off as the back door swung open and in walked Paulie and Al. They were carrying what appeared to be the remains of some tires.

"We were right behind them," Paulie said. "And the next thing I know, all four of my tires blew out. They had nails in them. I think she scattered those nails on purpose."

"You think?" Sal asked, rubbing one of his blue eyebrows.

Just then, Tate's phone sounded its distinctive James Bond chime.

"Base here," he answered. "What? She did what? Well, how did she get that much shaving cream in your car?"

The brothers exchanged glances. Mel had to turn away before she offended them all by laughing out loud.

"Well, fine. Go home then." He pressed a button on his phone and slid it back into his pocket. "I can't believe that six grown men can't manage to follow their little sister on a date without her knowing. You should all be ashamed of yourselves."

"Sal, Tony, what's the matter?" Joe De-Laura asked his brothers as he strolled in from the front room. "You look a little blue."

"Funny, really funny," Sal said. He jammed the rest of his cupcake into his mouth and stormed towards the door. "Let's go, Tony. I suppose you two need a ride?"

Without a word, Paulie and Al followed.

"I'm calling her cell phone," Tate said, and he strode back into the bakery.

"What did I miss?" Joe asked.

"Angie recon," Mel said. "It didn't go well."

Joe pulled her into his arms for a proper hello. When he released her, Mel had to steady herself by gripping the side of the table. Joe gave her a slow grin and then helped himself to an Orange Dreamsicle Cupcake.

"Heaven," he muttered through a bite of cupcake.

"Are you just dating me for my cupcakes?"

"Who said I was talking about the cupcake?" he countered. His dark brown eyes lingered on her face, and Mel felt herself flush. Oh, dear.

"I wish Angie were here," she said, feeling a sudden need to change the subject. "I'm

147

worried."

"Sounds like the brothers kept her too busy to get into trouble," Joe said. "Do you think she's in any danger?"

"From Roach?" Mel asked. "I don't know. I wish he wasn't Malloy's son, and I wish he wasn't a suspect."

"Me, too," Joe agreed. His voice was grim.

"Tate and I are going to the concert with Angie tonight," Mel said. She put her hand on Joe's shoulder to reassure him. "I'll check him out up close."

Joe put his hand over Mel's. "I don't like it. Promise me you'll be careful and call me before, during, and after, got it?"

"Got it."

"I have to get back to the office," he said with a sigh. "Don't forget. Call me."

He kissed Mel good-bye and left through the back door.

"I hope I'm not interrupting anything," a voice said from the opposite door.

Mel spun around to find Detective Martinez standing there. She had the feeling he'd been there watching them, and it irked her.

"Just saying good-bye to my boyfriend," she said.

"Assistant District Attorney Joe DeLaura," he said. "Nice."

"Is there a problem with me dating him?"

"Not for me," he said. He strolled around her kitchen and stopped at her industrial mixer. "Nice Hobart."

"Thanks."

"So, that was quite a luncheon this afternoon," he said.

Mel blew out a breath. So that's why he was here. She decided to play it cool. "Really? How so?"

"I heard there was quite a scuffle between you and Olivia Puckett."

"She's very territorial and has some issues with my bakery," Mel said.

"The way she told it, you cut into her charity event," he said.

"I covered for her," Mel said. "I teach a couples' cupcake class, and one of the women is on the board. I was happy to help out."

Wow, Mel thought. *Word choice is so very important when you are trying to avoid culpability without actually lying.*

"Ms. Puckett seemed to think you set it up," he said.

"I expect she was distraught at being late."

Detective Martinez turned back around to face her and crossed his arms over his chest. He resembled a brick wall. With his dark hair, dark eyes, dark skin, and sturdy

149

build, Mel had no doubt that he was very successful at intimidating his suspects. Fortunately, she was not one of them. She just had to keep reminding herself of that.

"Yes, that must be it," he said. Mel glanced away but felt him watching her.

Not a suspect, not a suspect, not a suspect. She chanted the litany in her head. Still, her palms were sweaty, and she felt the need to flee.

"Can I offer you a cupcake?" she asked.

"No th . . ." He paused and then said, "Actually, yes."

Mel was momentarily caught off guard. She had not figured him for a sweets guy and had just assumed he'd say no.

"Okay," she said.

This would take some thought. She looked him up and down. His khaki pants were pressed with a stiff crease, his shoes were buffed to a gloss that would allow her to check her teeth for stray lettuce leaves, and his dress shirt was wrinkle free and starched at the collar and cuffs. This was a man who paid attention to the details.

"Lemon," she said.

He raised his eyebrows.

"Sit," she said. "I'll be right back."

Mel ducked into the bakery and came back with a fresh lemon cupcake iced with a tart lemon buttercream. Milk didn't go very well with this one, so she poured him a glass of sweet tea to wash it down.

Martinez studied her. "How did you know?"

"Know what?" she asked.

"That lemon is my favorite flavor?"

Mel took the seat across from him. "I just had a feeling."

He cautiously sampled a small bite. His eyebrows lifted again, but this time in surprise.

"Wow," he said. "You made this?"

Mel nodded.

"Impressive," he said. He tucked into the cake and didn't speak again until it was gone and he'd drained his glass of iced tea. "Thank you."

"You're welcome," she said.

He picked up his plate and stood to take it to the sink. Mel stood at the same time, and they collided at the corner of the table. Martinez was reaching out to grab her elbow to steady her when the kitchen door swung open.

"Mel, what are you doing?" Tate stuck his head around the door. "We have to go! Angie, the concert, remember?"

"Concert?" Martinez asked.

"We're going to see a friend of a friend,

151

sort of," she said.

"Uh-huh." He studied her for a second and then said, "Have fun."

He strolled back out to the bakery, picking up a four-pack of lemon cupcakes on his way. As soon as Tate rang up the sale, he bolted the door after the detective and Mel was given no time to debate what the heck *that* had been about, which was probably a good thing. Because she definitely did not want to acknowledge the flutter of attraction she had felt when she and the detective collided. Nope, she wasn't going there. No way, no how.

"Mel, snap out of it!" Tate barked.

They scrambled around the bakery closing up, and Mel had just ditched her apron and changed her outfit when a car and driver pulled up to the curb.

"Show time," Tate said. He had a manic light in his eyes that made Mel nervous.

"So, what do we know about this guy exactly?" Tate asked Mel as they were driven to the Dodge Theater in downtown Phoenix in the Lincoln Town Car that Roach had sent for them. Angie was supposed to be with them, but she had texted Mel earlier that she'd meet them at the gig.

"He's Baxter Malloy's son, he and his father haven't spoken in years, and he likes

Angie," Mel said for the third time. She was getting tired of repeating herself.

"But why does he like Angie?" Tate asked. "He could have anyone. Why is he interested in a cupcake baker?"

"You should probably ask him," Mel suggested. She was beginning to lose her patience. "All I know is when Angie gave him static for coming after me, he was smitten. Probably, he's not used to women who don't fall all over themselves for him."

"So, it's just a phase that will pass?" Tate asked.

"Or it's the real thing," Mel said.

Tate glowered at the back of their driver's head.

"She's meeting us, right?"

"Yes," Mel answered. They'd covered this, too. "At the back entrance."

"Good." He folded his arms across his chest and brooded. Mel heaved a sigh. She wished Joe was here. It would have been nice to have his input right now, but he had to work on the trial. She knew it was the biggest case of his career — and she wanted him to succeed, she really did — but sometimes she felt like she had an absentee boyfriend.

"We're here," the driver said as he pulled around the back. He parked in a narrow spot between two black tour buses and hopped out to open the door for Mel and Tate.

"Ms. Cooper? Mr. Harper?" a man wearing an earpiece and looking harried approached them with two black lanyards that sported a plastic-encased picture of the band and listed them as VIPs.

"This way, please," he said.

Mel and Tate followed him up a staircase and through a heavy steel door. They were ushered down a hallway and led into a cramped room that smelled of incense.

The room was packed with people, and Mel craned her neck to see over the group. She needn't have bothered. A much taller Angie waved at them over the crowd. She kissed Roach on the cheek and made her way towards them.

"Isn't this hot?" she shouted over the crowd.

Mel was speechless. Petite Angie was five inches taller in red patent leather platform pumps that made her legs seem as if they stopped at her neck, a black micro-mini-skirt, and a white gauze shirt over a red bra. Her hair was big, her makeup was heavy, and she looked nothing like the former elementary school teacher they used to know.

TWELVE

" 'Dozens of people spontaneously combust each year. It's just not really widely reported,' " Tate said out of the side of his mouth to Mel.

"I heard that! *This Is Spinal Tap,*" Angie said, identifying the quote. "Very funny."

Mel glanced down at her jeans, high-heeled sandals and silk Alfani blouse and felt like she might as well be wearing a muumuu.

"You look fine," Angie said, as if reading her mind. "I'm just trying out the part of the rock-and-roll girlfriend."

"Girlfriend?" Tate choked out the word. "Isn't it a little premature to be labeling this fling as if it's a relationship?"

"Fling?" Angie asked with a laugh. "Let me assure you, this is no fling. Come and meet Roach."

Tate looked as if he might stroke out, so Mel braced him by putting her hand on his elbow and steering him through the crowd after Angie.

Roach was grinding on an enormous meatball sub. He had a gaggle of groupies around him, but he pushed them aside and pulled Angie up close against him.

"Hi, Mel," he said. "Hi, Todd."

"Tate."

Mel glanced at Tate, and his cold stare matched his tone of voice. She was surprised Roach didn't have frostbite.

"Sorry, man," Roach said and held out his hand. Tate shook it grudgingly. "Do you two want anything to eat? I have to load up before the show. Playing drums for two hours will wipe you out if you don't eat."

"No, thanks," Mel said.

"We're good," Tate agreed.

There was an awkward pause, and Angie looked between them as if hoping there'd be a spontaneous group hug. Mel could have told her not to hold her breath. Judging by the glower on Tate's face, the only thing he wanted to hug was Roach's neck between his hands.

"I got to sit in on the rehearsal today," Angie said. "It was boss."

Boss? Tate and Mel exchanged a look.

"Yo, Roach!" a tall skinny guy, who Mel recognized as the lead singer, yelled. "We have a schedule meeting with Jimbo."

"On my way," he said. He picked up his sandwich and kissed Angie on the cheek. "Why don't you go grab your seats? I'll meet you back here after the show."

"Okay!" Angie said. "Um . . . break a leg."

Roach tossed his black hair over his shoulder and grinned at her. "You are so cute."

With another kiss, he disappeared into the crowd.

"All right, just what the he—"

Mel cut off Tate's tirade before it could begin. "Who's Jimbo?"

"He's their manager," Angie said. "Roach calls him the warden."

"I need a drink," Tate muttered.

"There's a bar over here," Angie said. "Follow me."

They wound their way through the crowd towards a corner bar. Mel ordered a glass of wine, while Tate had a whiskey straight up and Angie had a beer.

It was too loud to talk, so Angie led them up the stairs towards the main theater, where they found their seats front and center, three rows back from the stage.

As they worked their way to their seats, a woman stepped in front of Angie and planted her hands on her hips in a fair imitation of a Jersey barrier.

An overprocessed bottle blonde with a long face, fake boobs, and bloodred nails, she looked like something that would crawl out of a basement on a moonlit night.

"Well, if it isn't the flavor of the month. You know you're just a shiny new toy for Roach, right? He's going to get tired of you, and he's going to kick your butt to the curb as soon as he's had his fill." She looked Angie up and down. "Which shouldn't take very long. Word of advice? Don't get too comfortable in my seat."

Angie gave her a withering stare. "You are so not talking to me."

"Oh, yes, I am," the woman said. She moved into Angie's personal space and poked her with one of her talons. Bad idea.

Mel and Tate exchanged an alarmed glance, but before they could intercept, Angie did a sweep kick into the other woman's left knee. The poor thing crumpled like a folding chair onto the theater floor.

"Meet the curb," Angie said and stepped over the other woman to continue on her way.

They settled into their seats with Tate in between them.

"I guess you'd better get used to that sort of thing," he said. "You know, having groupies crawling all over your boyfriend and getting in your face, since you're dating a rock star and all."

"You're right. I'm going to need to brush up on my kick-boxing," Angie said. Then she grinned. "Man, this is going to be fun."

Tate frowned; obviously that was not the reaction he had anticipated.

"Nice kick, Ange," a guy in a black T-shirt with electrical cords wrapped around his arm shouted from the stage. "Anyone who can take down Clarisse is okay in my book. I knew I liked you."

"Thanks, Carl," she said. "Hey, these are my friends Mel and Tate."

They waved, and Carl jumped off the stage to shake hands.

"Roach says Carl is the best equipment man in the biz," Angie said.

Carl laughed. "Well, you're all in for a treat tonight. The band hasn't played in over a week, so they are going to blow the doors off of this place."

"Excuse me." Angie pulled her phone out of her pocket, checked the caller ID, and turned away to answer it.

"They haven't had a show in over a week?" Mel asked. "I thought these tours went from city to city with no breaks?"

"Usually they do, but the guys wanted

some downtime, and then that . . . uh . . . thing with Roach's dad happened, so we haven't played since Vegas."

"So they've just been practicing?" Tate asked.

Carl burst out laughing. "Man, these guys are pros. They don't need to practice. They could be half-dead and moving towards the light, but if you put a guitar in their hands, they'd start playing."

"So, they don't even rehearse?" Mel asked.

"Nah, only if one of them writes a new song," he said.

"Anything new lately?" Mel asked.

"No, just Ange, and she is the coolest," Carl gushed. "Well, I'd better hustle. Enjoy the show."

"Thanks," they said together.

Mel glanced past Tate. Angie was still on the phone and had her back turned towards them.

"He lied," she hissed to Tate.

"Who? Carl?"

"No, Roach," she said. "He told Angie and me that he was at rehearsal the evening his father was killed."

Tate's eyes about popped out of his head. He opened his mouth to tell Angie, but Mel put her hand on his arm.

"No, not yet," she said. "We only have

Carl's information. We need confirmation before we say anything to Angie."

"I disagree. We have to tell her now," he said.

"Tell me what?"

Tate and Mel turned to see Angie looking at them.

" 'When we go to Morocco, I think we should have completely different names and be completely different people,' " Mel said.

Almost Famous," Angie said, identifying the quote with a grin. "Wow, you two are really banging out the rock-and-roll movie quotes. Hey, does that make me Penny Lane?"

"No!" Tate said, frowning. "Absolutely not."

Angie gave him a one-armed hug. "Relax, I'm just joshing."

His frown deepened.

Mel glanced at her watch. The concert was going to start in twenty minutes. If she was going to find out if Roach had lied, she had to do it now.

She drained her plastic wine glass and rose from her seat.

"I'm going to get another," she said. "Anyone need one? Okay, be right back."

She realized that she hadn't given them time to answer, but that was for the best, given that she wasn't going to the bar anyway.

She flashed her badge at a security guard and hurried down the stairs back to the green room where the band congregated. A few of the roadies were eating, but no one took notice of her as she wandered through the room.

Now that she was here, she wasn't really sure who she could ask questions. Would anyone talk to her? And even if they did, how would she know if they were telling the truth?

She needed access to their schedule. If only there was a master calendar posted to the wall or something she could check to find out where Roach was on the night his father had been killed.

"What are *you* doing down here?" Clarisse, the blonde Angie had deposited on the ground, was hobbling across the room, holding an ice pack to her backside.

"Looking for Jimbo," Mel said. "Roach sent me."

Now where had that lie come from? She had to admit it was a good one. If anyone knew Roach's whereabouts it would be his manager, right?

Clarisse glared at her as she filled a plate from the buffet. "Well, duh, he's obviously

162

up in the sound booth where he always sits."

"Oh, yeah," Mel said. She hurried to the door. She only had ten minutes until show-time.

"Excuse me, ma'am, do you belong here?" A very large security guard stopped her by putting out his arm.

"Yep," Mel said and flashed her badge. "You may want to get rid of that blonde over there, though. She's eating all the food, and she's not with the band."

She heard a yelp behind her but didn't turn around to see what had happened to the obnoxious Clarisse. She raced back out to the theater. The sound booth was at the back of the lower-level seating.

Mel hurried over to it and glanced at the three men standing at the controls. One was short, round, and balding. She was betting he was Jimbo.

She waved at him, and he looked behind him to see if she was signaling someone else. She gestured for him to come talk to her and saw him say something to the other men before he joined her.

"You really need to get to your seat, miss. The show is about to start," he said.

"I know," Mel said. "But I need to ask you something. You're Jimbo, right?"

"Yeah," he said. "Why?"

"I'm trying to find out what the band's favorite flavor of cupcakes are. I work with Roach's new friend Angie, and we want to bake a big batch for all of you."

"Well, now that's nice of you," he said. "Could we do it after the show, though, when we've got more time?"

"Oh, well, we heard you all practice every day, and we wanted to get baking tonight, so you'll have them for your practice tomorrow," Mel said.

"Practice?" he laughed. "Honey, the only practice these boys do is floating on their backsides in the pool at the hotel. These guys are pros. They don't practice."

"Not ever?" Mel asked, feeling her chest squeeze tight.

"Never," he confirmed. The lights in the theater dimmed. "Tell you what. Make a variety of flavors, and we'll all be happy."

"Okay," Mel said. She forced the corners of her lips to curve up and turned to hurry back to her seat. This confirmed it. Roach had lied. Mel felt queasy, thinking of Angie dating a killer.

A low buzz of excitement began to hum throughout the theater. The lights went out. The last of the incoming audience scrambled to their seats.

Mel realized the last time she'd been to

the Dodge was to see Blondie. She wondered if the Sewers would command the stage as well.

She needn't have worried. A lone light from above the stage lit an enormous drum set, and there was Roach, shirtless and tapping his snare in a steady cadence. The crowd sat mesmerized, waiting for what would come next.

Mel was riveted by the powerful ripple of the muscles in his arms. It would have been so easy for him to strangle his father with such upper-body strength.

Roach tossed his head, and his long black hair flowed down behind his back. His tattoos came to life with every flex of his muscles, causing a collective sigh to be emitted by the female members of the crowd. Roach looked up. His light blue eyes scanned the crowd until they found Angie. He gave her a wicked grin and then winked at her.

Angie beamed back at him and, as if it was a secret signal between the two of them, Roach exploded into a blur of motion and his drums burst into a thunderous beat that called the rest of the band out onto the stage.

They played two hours of nonstop, pulse-pounding rock and roll. By the time they left the stage after their third encore, Mel was relieved to see them go. Her legs hurt, her back hurt, and she was pretty sure she'd lost her voice.

They waited for the crowd to disperse and then trailed back down the stairs. They flashed their VIP badges at the posted security guards and joined the band in the green room.

As soon as Angie stepped into the room, Roach snatched her up and hugged her close. He planted a kiss on her and then stepped back to study her face.

"What did you think?"

"I loved it," Angie gushed. "You're a god."

He laughed and pulled her close again. Tucking her against his side, he noticed Mel and Tate. "Hi, Mel. Hey there, Tim."

"Tate."

"We're all going out for a bite," Roach said. "Do you want to join us?"

"No," Tate said. He took Angie's elbow and gently tried to pry her out of Roach's arms. "And you have to be up early tomorrow for a business meeting."

"What business meeting?" she asked. She shook him off and pressed herself back against Roach.

"We have to go over our quarterly statements," Tate said.

With her ears ringing like they'd been slapped repeatedly by trash can lids, Mel was only catching every other word. Still, she wondered if Tate thought he was fooling anyone.

"No, we don't," Angie argued. "What do you think, Mel? Are you up for dinner?"

"Huh?" Mel asked. "I'm pretty much lipreading here. You have to speak up."

Roach busted up laughing. "I like you, Mel. You're a gas."

"Eat," Angie shouted. "Do you want to?"

"Bed," Mel said with a shake of her head. "All I want is bed."

"Okay, I'll see you two tomorrow then," Angie said.

"The car will take you home," Roach said. "Thanks for coming to the show."

He swung Angie into the crowd, and the two of them were swallowed up in a sea of high fives and backslaps.

"You couldn't back me up, there?" Tate chided Mel as they trudged out the back door.

"Did you really think she was going to leave her new boyfriend to go to bed early because you want to go over the quarterlies tomorrow?" Mel asked.

"Boyfriend?" Tate's voice rose an octave. "I don't see him as her boyfriend."

Mel gave him a hard stare. The driver was waiting at the edge of the lot with the back passenger door open.

"Come on," she said. "We need to talk."

In the blessed silence of the backseat, Mel studied Tate as the driver weaved his way through the city streets back to South Scottsdale. By unspoken mutual agreement, neither of them spoke until the driver let them out at the bakery.

"Angie is out with a man who could very well have murdered his own father," Tate said.

"I am fully aware of the situation," Mel said. She walked down the narrow alley and unlocked the back door to the bakery kitchen. Tate followed. "But seriously, a business meeting was the best thing you could come up with?"

"What? It was perfectly reasonable," he said.

Mel slammed her purse down on the table and turned to face Tate. "It was lame."

"At least I tried," he said. "You let her go."

"Because we need to talk," Mel said. "Listen, I talked to Jimbo, the band's manager, and he confirmed that there haven't been any practices. So, it's official that Roach was not at practice that night like he said."

"So where was he the night his father died?" Tate demanded.

"I don't know, but I don't like this."

"And you let her go eat dinner with him?" he yelled. "I hate this. I hate that she's out with him and I hate that he's probably a murderer."

"Tate, relax," Mel said. "We need to come up with a plan."

"Don't tell me to relax," he snapped. He looked like he was at the end of his rope, and Mel wondered if he was finally getting it.

"Tate, why do you suppose it bothers you so much that Angie is dating him?"

"Because he's a killer," Tate retorted. "And she's my friend. I'd be equally upset if you were dating a killer."

"No, you wouldn't," Mel said.

Tate gasped in outrage. "Yes, I would."

"Listen, I know jealous when I see jealous," Mel said. "You are jealous."

"I am not," he protested.

"Yeah, you are," she said.

"Am not."

"Are, too."

"Am —" he began, but Mel cut him off.

"Oh, forget it! If you can't figure out why this bothers you so much, then you really are hopeless."

"Am n—" he began, but Mel held up her hand and ordered, "Don't say it."

"So, what are we going to do?" he asked. "She's out there with a probable murderer."

Mel lifted her car keys off of the hook on the wall.

"Come on, we're going on a stakeout."

"Seriously?"

"Do you have a better idea?"

"Short of backing over him with my car? No."

"Then let's go."

" 'Ma'am, what is the approximate dry weight of the average Madagascan fruit tree bat?' " Tate asked in his best Joe Friday voice.

"*Dragnet,* really?" Mel asked. She rolled her eyes and led the way out the door.

THIRTEEN

"Stakeouts are not as exciting as they sound," Tate said.

"What do you know?" Mel asked. "You've been asleep for the past half hour."

"I was just resting my eyes," he said.

"Do you always drool when you're just resting your eyes?"

"It's a salivary condition."

"Uh-huh."

Tate stretched and yawned. He was six feet tall and pushing two hundred pounds. Mel felt herself lean over to give him more room. Why was it all of the men in her life seemed to take up too much space? Specifically, *her* space.

They were parked two houses down from Angie's duplex in the neighborhood just south of Old Town Scottsdale. Rectangular brick houses built on slabs, they'd probably popped up in 1959 like fruit on a prickly pear cactus.

"What did you mean when you said I was jealous?" Tate asked.

"That's not self-explanatory?" she asked.

He shrugged. "I'm just protective of you two, that's all."

"Deny, deny, deny," Mel said. "How's that working for you?"

"For me?" he asked. "How's it working for you and Joe? Are you ever going to get horizontal with him?"

Mel sucked in a breath. "We get horizontal all the time."

"I'm not talking about unconscious horizontal," he said.

"What makes you think we haven't been . . . conscious?"

"Oh, puleeeze," Tate said. "I know you. Every time you get intimate with a guy you go on a baking bender."

"I do not. . . . I do?"

"Three months dating Gary the barista and you created the Espresso-Shot Cupcake. Five months with the geologist from the university and you came up with the Crystal Cupcake."

"Oh, yeah, we decorated the cupcakes with rock candy," Mel said. "Those were cool."

"See? That's how I know you and Joe have not gotten naked together yet."

"You can sleep with someone without being naked," Mel said.

"Yeah, if you're talking asleep-sleeping with someone," he said. He leaned back against the passenger door and studied her. "What's the holdup anyway? You've been in love with him since we were kids."

"You knew?"

He just looked at her, and Mel let out a pent-up sigh. "It's this stupid case of his — not that the case is stupid. It's huge. It's just taking up all of his time, and when I do see him . . ."

"He's dead tired?"

"Out before the light."

"Bummer," Tate said.

"Yeah." Given the direction of the conversation, Mel figured it was a good time to put to rest Angie's suspicions once and for all. "So, it doesn't bother you that I'm dating him?"

"Well, honestly . . ." he began, but then he swore and crouched down, dragging Mel with him. "Get down! It's them!"

A moving headlight illuminated the inside of the car. Mel wondered if Angie recognized it. It was a classic red-and-white Mini Cooper, so it wasn't unique, but still, Angie might be suspicious if she saw it parked on her street. Nuts, she should have parked farther away.

"What should we do?" she asked.

"Poke your head up, and see if you see her," he said. "See if he's with her."

"Me? You do it."

"You're her best friend," he said.

"So are you," she argued.

"It's your car."

"I knew we should have taken your car," Mel said. "What if she saw us? She'll be furious."

"She didn't see us."

"How do you know?"

The theme from *Gone with the Wind* flowed from Mel's purse.

Still hunched over, she and Tate looked at each other in alarm.

"Are you expecting a call at one in the morning?" Tate asked.

"It could be Joe," she said and fished the phone out of her bag. "Uh-oh, it's Angie."

"Maybe she's just reporting on her date," Tate said. "Bluff."

"Hello?" Mel answered, trying to sound as if she'd just woken up.

"Don't bother," Angie said. "I see you. You know, if you want to be discreet, you really need to take the cupcake antenna ball off your car."

"Damn. I'm sorry, Ange."

"What?" Tate whispered. "What did she say? Is she okay? Did he hurt her?"

"Chillax," Mel whispered. "She's fine, but she sees us."

"Oh." Tate sat back in his seat.

"Roach just left," Angie said. "Why don't you two come in for some breakfast?"

"At one in the morning?" Mel asked.

"Sure, it'll be like old times."

"On our way," Mel said. She shut her phone and started up her car. She pulled into Angie's small driveway and parked behind her Honda sedan.

Angie was standing in the doorway that led from her carport to her kitchen. Tate and Mel approached with caution.

"Are you mad?" Mel asked.

"Nah," Angie said. "I know what you're worried about, but you're wrong. Roach didn't hurt his father. I know it."

"How can —" Tate began, but Mel interrupted, finishing his sentence: "— you stand all those groupies?"

Angie looked at them and then pointed to her outfit. "You're kidding, right? I think I am now the queen of the groupies."

"So, where is he?" Tate asked between his teeth.

"Roach has to get up early for an interview, so we called it an early night."

A slow grin spread across Tate's face.

"What are you smiling about?" Angie asked.

"Nothing," he said. "It's just a nice night out tonight."

Angie glanced between them and then raised her eyebrows in question at Mel, who shrugged.

"Come on," Angie said, stepping aside to let them in. "I'll make you two some eggs."

Angie flipped on the radio, and they grooved to a jazz station while they made toast, scrambled eggs, and ham. The kitchen was warm on the cold night, and the old-fashioned aqua-tiled counters were welcoming, as if they'd just been waiting for friends to gather round.

Mel watched as Tate teased Angie about her big hair. Angie laughed with him, but something had changed. Angie wasn't looking at Tate like she used to, with her heart in her eyes. Mel wondered if Tate noticed the difference.

He seemed to be putting forth an even greater effort to make Angie laugh, so Mel figured he did notice the difference, even if it was on an unconscious level. Then she wondered when Tate would realize that he was in love with Angie. He was a man, so it could take a while. She hoped, for his sake, that when he finally did figure it out, it wasn't too late.

"Aunt Mel, look at me!" a hip-high Darth Vader shouted as he waved a lightsaber at an equally short Luke Skywalker, who was racing away across Joyce's backyard.

"I'm looking," Mel yelled back and grinned. Her nephews had been battling each other all evening. She had even spent half an hour tied to an orange tree, pretending to be Princess Leia until Joe showed up and, in his best Han Solo impersonation, saved her. At which point he kissed her, making both boys gag and retch.

"I wish I had their energy," Joe said as the boys raced by again, making all sorts of loud lightsaber noises.

"No kidding," Mel said. They were sitting at her mother's patio table, having just finished dinner.

"It's all I can do to keep up with them," Charlie said from the hammock nearby.

"Ditto," said his wife, Nancy, who was sharing the hammock with him.

"Boys, cookies!" Joyce called from the doorway.

Darth and Luke turned on a dime and sped for the house.

"Wash your hands!" Nancy called after them.

"Aw, Mom, I just licked them clean," Darth Vader complained. "See?"

He dropped his lightsaber and held up two sticky hands for inspection. Nancy and Joyce exchanged a look that was equal parts maternal amusement and gross-out.

"Soap. Water. March," Joyce said.

"Aw, crud," Darth and Luke grumbled as the door shut behind them.

"Thanks for coming down with the boys," Mel said to Charlie and Nancy. "They've cheered Mom up tremendously."

"Exhausted her is more like it," Charlie said. "But we're happy to be here. So, do the police have any suspects?"

"You mean aside from Mom?" Mel asked.

"And my sister's new boyfriend?" Joe asked.

Mel and Joe linked hands. Neither one of them was happy about the Angie-Roach situation.

"They don't really suspect Mom, do they?" Nancy asked.

"I don't think so, but Detective Martinez stopped by the bakery yesterday, and I don't think it was to buy cupcakes — although he did," Mel said.

Joe sat up straighter. "You didn't tell me

about that."

"I didn't?" Mel asked. "Well, after last night's concert and staying up so late with Tate and Angie, my brain is a little fuzzy."

"I don't like this," Joe said. "I don't like Martinez sniffing around the shop."

"Well, it's not like he thinks Mel is a suspect," Charlie said. "I mean, you weren't even there, right?"

"There is the dress debacle," Mel said. "But no, I don't think he thinks I'm a suspect."

"Maybe he wants to date you," Nancy said and wiggled her eyebrows.

Mel glanced quickly at Joe, who glowered and said, "Sorry, you're off the market."

She grinned at him. Not that she had been worried or anything, but it was good to know that Joe was still in. Maybe tonight would be the night. She felt herself break into a sweat, and it wasn't from nerves.

An old-fashioned telephone ring sounded, and Joe fished his phone out of his pocket. He glanced at the screen.

"Sorry, it's the office," he said. He squeezed Mel's hand before letting go, and then strolled over to the edge of the yard to stand between her mother's orange trees.

"I'm going to go see if Mom needs help," Nancy said. "Our two Jedi Knights will be

179

covered in milk and cookies, and they're definitely going to need baths." She untangled herself from Charlie's arms and shook her long, dark hair free. She kissed his head as she climbed out of the hammock.

Charlie watched her go, and Mel could tell from the soft look in his eyes that he was as much in love with her today as he had been when he first fell for her in college, maybe even more so.

"Mel, I want to talk to you about Mom." Charlie sat up a little straighter.

"What's up?"

"I want her to come back to Flagstaff with us," he said.

"That's a great idea," Mel said. "It would do her some good."

"I found her pacing around the house last night at two in the morning. She was checking all of the doors and windows with a fire poker in one hand and a flashlight in the other," Charlie said. "I think she's afraid that the murderer is going to come after her."

"Have you seen anything that makes you think that?" Mel asked.

"No, nothing out of the ordinary has happened, but that doesn't mean she isn't right," Charlie said. "I mean, she was there when Malloy was strangled. The murderer has to be a little concerned that she might have seen something."

Mel fretted her lower lip between her teeth. "We should call Uncle Stan."

"I talked to him this morning," Charlie said. "If Mom refuses to come to Flagstaff with us, he's going to stay in the guest-house."

"You know she's going to refuse," Mel said.

"Yep. I know she thinks it will look bad, plus she'd be terrified that the boys would be put in danger."

Mel reached across the space between them and squeezed her brother's arm. "I promise I'll take good care of her."

"I know."

They were silent for a moment, sharing their worry for their mom. Then Charlie patted her hand, and Mel released him and leaned back in her chair.

"So, how's Joe?" Charlie asked. "Treating you right?"

"Of course," Mel said. "You know Joe. He's a perfect gentleman."

"A little too perfect?"

Mel frowned at her brother as he toed the ground with the front of his black Converse high-tops, keeping the hammock swaying.

"What's that supposed to mean?" she asked.

"Well, word on the street is that you two haven't had a chance to bump uglies yet," he said.

"Bump uglies? You did not just say that."

"Uh, yeah, I did."

"How is this any of your business?"

"Oh, don't get all wiggy," Charlie said. "I'm your brother. You can talk to me."

"There is nothing to talk about," Mel said. "The man has the biggest case of his career on the line, and he's working 24-7. Bumpin' uglies can wait."

"I don't think that sets a very good precedent for the long term," Charlie said.

Mel clapped her hands over her ears, "La-la-la-la. I'm so not having this conversation. La-la-la-la-la."

Mercifully, Darth Vader, who now resembled a boy, chose that moment to hurry out the back door for good-night hugs. Mel kissed his damp head and was pleased to see him scamper across the lawn to give Joe a good-night high five.

Joe winked at her, and she felt her heart lift. So what if everyone in the Valley of the Sun knew that they hadn't gotten horizontal yet. Heck, maybe she'd wait until she married him. Married him? Did she really just think that? Uh-oh.

She glanced up and found Joe watching her. She hurriedly looked away. It would not do for him to sense her thoughts had strayed anywhere near the *M* word. She knew men who would flee to Mexico without a passport if they thought the girl they were dating even entertained the idea of a white gown and a limo ride. Mel didn't know if Joe was one of those men, and until she knew, it would behoove her to play it cool. Act casual.

Luke Skywalker appeared before her, and Mel kissed his head, too. It wasn't enough, however, and he wriggled into her lap and demanded a story. He handed her a beat-up copy of *Curious George,* and she remembered her father reading it over and over and over again to her and Charlie when they were little.

She glanced at Joe, and he nodded, letting her know they had time for stories. She smiled and went in to read the two boys to sleep.

She tried not to think about what it would be like to have a child with Joe. Would it have his dark hair and warm brown eyes? Mrs. Joe DeLaura. *Eep.* She smacked her forehead with the book.

"What did you do that for, Aunt Mel?"

Darth Vader asked. He pushed his mask up onto the top of his head to get a good look at her.

"I was trying to smack some sense into myself," she said.

"Did it work?" Luke Skywalker asked.

"No, I don't recommend it," she said.

Both boys nodded, and Mel hugged them close. Well, if she couldn't be a role model for what to do, at least she could model what not to do. Story of her life.

"Okay," Mel said as she glanced at her reflection in the mirror. Joe was in the living room, waiting for her while she tried to make herself look presentable. Tonight was the night, she was sure of it. And it wasn't that she felt goaded on to the next level because everyone seemed to feel the need to comment on their lack of momentum in that direction. Not at all.

It was merely a good night for it. Valentine's Day was coming. There were hearts and flowers everywhere you looked. Love was in the air.

She adjusted the straps of her silky, pale blue nightie and ran her fingers through her short blonde hair. Her teeth were brushed; anything that needed to be shaved or plucked had been. She had spritzed herself with perfume, or, more accurately, she had spritzed the air and walked through it. She was as ready as she'd ever be.

Mel slowly opened the bathroom door and stepped out into her living room, which was also her bedroom. A grating sound like a logger working a chainsaw filled the room, followed by a rush of air.

Joe had one arm draped across the back of the futon and his other hand held the TV remote. He looked as if he'd been watching TV, and then his head had flopped back against the cushions. The man was as unconscious as a fighter who'd been KO'd.

Mel wondered if she should wake him up. But somehow it just seemed cruel, given how tired he was. She knew this case was giving him trouble. The defense attorneys were charging that the evidence had been tampered with, and they were out to discredit Joe's best witness. In sleep, the man had some peace. How could she disturb that?

She turned and went back to the bathroom, where she changed into her comfy pajamas. Then she went back out to the living room and pulled out the futon, shifting Joe as necessary. When she climbed in beside him, he wrapped his arms about her, and Mel smiled. Suddenly, she didn't care what anyone else thought. She and Joe had all the time in the world.

Mel awoke to a hot cup of coffee on the table by her head and a note. It was short and sweet, but it sent shivers down to her toes. Joe had better be able to put this shooter away and soon, or she was afraid she'd have to shoot him herself.

FOURTEEN

"You're going to have to fire her," Marty said. He was wearing a blue Fairy Tale Cupcake apron and wiping down the tables after a group of older ladies had flirted outrageously with him and eaten a dozen cupcakes.

"I can't fire my business partner," Mel said. "She's just late. She'll be here."

"She leaves early, shows up late or not at all," Marty said. Without his toupee, the remaining wisps of his hair stood up in indignation. He looked every inch the cranky old man. "What kind of partner is that?"

"She's going through something," Mel said. "We just have to give her some time."

He heaved a put-upon sigh. "She'd better get it together quickly. You're not going to have my free labor to bail you out after the contest."

"I appreciate your help," Mel said. "Angie

will come around. You'll see."

As if on cue, the front door opened and in strode Angie. "Sorry I'm late!"

"Two hours late, little missy," Marty chided her. "You'd better have a good excuse."

Angie looked from him to Mel. "I've been replaced?"

"Marty's helping me out for free raffle entries."

Angie glanced at the box. It was stuffed with slips.

"Wow, that contest was a good idea," she said. "Let me dump my stuff, and I'll grab the front. I know you need to prep for class tonight."

"Thanks," Mel said.

Angie vanished, and Marty plunked his hands on his hips and gave Mel an outraged stare. "You're not even going to ask her where she's been?"

"She'll tell me if she wants me to know," Mel said.

"You know she was with that musician," Marty said.

"Maybe," Mel said.

Marty lifted off his apron and tossed it down on the counter. "I'm late for yoga."

"So, you're just going to make like a vrksasana and leave?" she asked.

"Ha! Yoga tree pose . . . leave . . . very funny," Marty said. "How long have you been waiting to use that?"

"A while."

Marty ran a hand over his shiny dome. Mel guessed this was the first time he'd been to yoga without his rug.

She suspected he was nervous.

"You look fine," she said.

He scowled at her. "I know that. Don't you think I know that?"

He shuffled to the door.

"See you tomorrow," Mel called.

He gave her a curt wave and let the door bang shut behind him.

"Real ray of sunshine, isn't he?" Angie asked as she reentered the kitchen.

"He's growing on me," Mel said.

"Like fungus?" Angie asked.

"Hmm," Mel hummed. "So?"

"So what?" Angie asked. She stepped next to Mel and began off-loading cupcakes from a tray into the display case.

"Why were you late?"

"I slept late," Angie said. "Roach and I drove up to Jerome last night."

"Jerome?" Mel asked. "That's almost two hours away, and it's cold up there."

Angie grinned. "Yeah, it was so romantic. We ate dinner and then caught a local band called the Cartwheels at the Spirit Room."

"Sounds nice," Mel said. She was happy for Angie, she really was, but there was a part of her that was jealous of the unimpeded romance that she and Roach had going. It felt as if she and Joe had never had that opportunity.

Angie must have sensed what she was feeling. "Don't worry. As soon as Joe's case wraps up, you'll have this sort of time together."

"Maybe," Mel said. She was unconvinced. What if Joe's life was always this hectic? The thought was depressing.

"Shake it off," Angie said. "It will get better, I promise."

Mel shook her head. "You're right. I know you're right."

"Okay, so what are we cooking for our couples' class tonight?"

"A raspberry white chocolate cupcake that I call Cupid's Bliss."

"Did you just make that name up?" Angie asked.

"Yeah. Too much?"

"Normally, I would say yes, but it is the season of love," Angie said. "The cornier the better."

"I didn't think it was corny, exactly," Mel said.

"Well, it is," Angie said. "Still, white chocolate and raspberry, what's not to love?"

"Exactly," Mel said.

They set to work. Because of the high sugar content in the white chocolate, Mel decided to make smaller cupcakes and bake them longer at a lower temperature. Twenty minutes at 325 degrees kept them from over-browning, and the tops came out flatter, which worked out fine. Using a star tip, Mel piped white chocolate–cream cheese icing around the edge of the cupcake, connecting one end of the circle to the other.

Angie carefully placed fresh raspberries inside the white chocolate ring, making sure the bottoms were all facing up. Mel then drizzled a red raspberry glaze over the berries and the white chocolate icing.

"Oh, wow. Can I have one?" a voice asked from the doorway.

Mel turned and there was Detective Martinez. He looked as buttoned-down as ever in charcoal gray slacks and a white dress shirt. Today, he was even wearing a tie.

"Sure, Detective," Mel said. She plated one of the cupcakes for him and gestured for him to sit down.

Angie glanced between them and then hefted the tray of remaining cupcakes and headed for the walk-in cooler.

"So, how was that concert?" he asked.

"Concert?" Mel asked.

"The last time I was here, you and your partner Tate were headed for a concert." He tucked his fork into the cupcake and scooped up a bite with cake, icing, and a raspberry.

"Oh, yeah," she said. She glanced nervously at the cooler. What would Angie make of this? "We went to see the Sewers. It was great."

"Brian Malloy is in that band, isn't he?"

"Yes, he is," Angie said. Obviously, she had heard the entire conversation from the depths of the enormous refrigerator. "And yes, he is Baxter's son, and yes, they were estranged, and yes, I am dating him."

Martinez looked surprised.

"Oh, you didn't know that, did you?" Angie asked. Her face grew red, and she fidgeted with her apron pockets. "We just started dating a few days ago."

Martinez took another bite of cupcake. "This is amazing."

"Thanks," Mel said. Her throat felt dry, and she coughed. She had a bad feeling about this conversation.

"How did you two meet?" Martinez asked.

"He came here to talk to Mel," Angie said.

"He thought I was my mother," Mel explained. "He thought I had something to do with his father's death."

"Why would he think that?"

Mel shrugged. "He was angry. He thought I was a gold digger."

"How did he react when he found out you weren't the one dating his father?"

"He was embarrassed and apologetic."

Martinez finished off the cupcake.

"How did you come to be dating him?" Martinez asked Angie as he took his plate to the sink and rinsed it.

"He asked me," she said.

"You are aware he's a murder suspect." Martinez turned away from the sink and studied Angie with concern.

"He didn't do it," she said. "He's a musician, not a killer."

"Don't fool yourself," Martinez said. "I once had a case where a Sunday-school teacher chopped up her husband and put him in the freezer because he kept leaving his underwear on the bathroom floor."

"Well, that would grate after a while," Angie said.

Martinez frowned. The jangle of the bells on the front door sounded from the front room, and Angie said, "I'll get that" as she hurried out of the kitchen.

"Do you think Roach is guilty?" Mel asked. She wondered if she should mention what the roadie, Carl, and the manager, Jimbo, had said, that Roach hadn't been rehearsing on the night of his father's murder. She wondered if she should tell him that Roach had lied to them. Had he lied to the police, too? If Martinez said yes, she was so going to tell and pull the plug on Angie's new romance.

"I don't know," Martinez said. "He certainly had motive."

"Who had motive?" a voice asked from the door.

They both turned, and Mel started in surprise when Steve Wolfmeier strode into the room. Wearing a perfectly tailored Brook Brothers suit and Gucci loafers, he reeked of high-profile attorney, and Mel knew just from looking at Martinez's face that he knew exactly who Steve was: the most successful defense attorney in the Valley of the Sun.

"Hi, Melanie," Steve said. "Long time, no see."

Martinez glanced from her to Steve and back again. He did not look happy.

"Hi, Steve," Mel said. "What brings you here?"

"Cupcakes, naturally," he said. He opened

194

his hands wide in a trusting gesture she was sure had been well rehearsed before hundreds of jurors. She noticed that the lower button on the jacket of his pinstripe suit was unbuttoned as if he were a male model and she wanted to laugh. The man simply had no self-esteem issues. Not a one. "Why else would I be here?"

"Why else indeed," Martinez said with a shake of his head. He turned and looked at Mel. "Thanks for the cupcake. I'll be in touch."

They watched as Martinez strode out of the room.

"Oh, don't tell me I chased away the good-looking detective?" Steve asked.

"I think he might be allergic to you," she said.

"They all are," he said with a grin. "But seriously, what's with the stiff? I thought you were dating DeLaura."

"How do you know that?" she asked.

"I have my sources," he said. "So, are you or aren't you?"

"I am," she said.

"Pity," he said. He glanced at her from beneath his lashes.

"Yeah, right." Mel couldn't help but laugh. "So, why are you *really* here?"

"I read about your mother's unfortunate

situation in the *Republic* and I wanted to see if there was anything I could do to help." He ran a manicured hand through his short, prematurely gray hair. Instead of making him look older, it made him look distinguished, and Mel was pretty sure he knew it.

"Really?" she asked. "Is business that slow?"

"Ouch," he said. He put a hand over his chest. "You cut me to the quick."

"Sorry, just trying to cut through the BS."

"You don't like me much, do you?" he asked as he leaned against the table.

"I like you fine," she said. "I just don't trust you."

"But you do like me," he said with a wicked grin. "That's an excellent start."

Mel found herself laughing again. Steve Wolfmeier was known as the best defense attorney in town because he generally left his opponent in shreds. Nice to see he had an equal amount of charm to offer.

"My mother isn't going to need an attorney," she said. "She's innocent."

"Ah, but now your best friend is dating the prime suspect," he said.

"Again, how do you know these things?"

"I told you, I have my sources," he said. "And I was eavesdropping."

196

"Now it's all coming into focus. You're hoping we'll hook you up with Roach Malloy?"

"Big celebrity, very high profile. You still have my card, right?" he asked.

"Unbelievable."

"I know. Now, let's talk cupcakes," he said.

He left just before Mel's class was to begin with a dozen cupcakes, one in every flavor.

FIFTEEN

Per usual, the Bickersons arrived first. Irene huffed into the kitchen, obviously put out with Dan — again.

"A *gentle*man would open a door for a lady," she berated him. "Not let it slam in her face."

"It slipped," Dan said.

"Well, it wouldn't have if you'd let me go first, like a person with manners and not some barnyard animal."

"If the sow fits," he returned.

Irene puffed out her cheeks. Her chubby face was becoming an alarming shade of red, and Mel and Angie glanced at each other, wondering how to head off the impending ruckus when the kitchen door swung open and in walked the rest of the class.

The Felixes, the Dunns, and the Koslowskis arrived, followed by Jay and Poppy Gatwick. As they greeted one another, the atmosphere in the room began to mellow, and the red receded from Irene's cheeks.

Angie worked one side of the table while Mel worked the other. The white chocolate batter was scooped into the industrial-size cupcake tins and placed in the oven.

The class took a short break while the cupcakes baked. Most of the couples went out the front door to stretch their legs and window-shop in Old Town. Poppy ducked into the shop's small restroom while Jay waited.

Angie's cell phone rang with a song from the Sewers and, with a big grin, she slipped out the back to take the call, which was undoubtedly Roach. Mel wondered what level their relationship had gotten to, since Angie had changed her ringtone for him. That seemed awfully serious, and she couldn't help but acknowledge she had never done that for Joe.

Mel took the free time to clean up the dirty bowls, cooking implements, and batter splatters before they started on the icing for the second half of the class.

"How's your mother, Melanie?" Jay asked as he helped put the bowls in the sink.

"She's all right," Mel said. "My brother is in town, and that's keeping her occupied."

"Good," he said. "Poppy has been so

199

distraught. She seems to think there is a strangler on the loose and is afraid to be alone. I tried to tell her it wasn't a random act of violence, but she's still afraid."

A vision of Baxter Malloy's body crossed through Mel's mind, and she had to agree with Poppy. The thought that someone was capable of strangling another human being to death was horrifying.

"I don't blame her," Mel said with a shudder.

"I want you to know," Jay said, "that I've been listening for any snippet of information that might be of help."

"Have you heard anything?" Mel asked. She put her bowls in the sink and turned to face him. She knew it would relieve her mother's mind if there was a solid suspect out there.

"The list of people who lost money in Baxter's scheme is daunting," Jay said. "And yet . . ."

"Yet?" Mel encouraged him.

"I keep coming back to the Hargraves," Jay said. "Can you imagine what it must have been like to lose billions?"

"No, I really can't," Mel said. She felt terrible for the older couple, truly. "But you don't think Lester could have harmed Baxter do you? The man must be at least eighty."

"He's eighty exactly," Jay said. "A depression baby, going out the same way he came in. That has to be tough."

"But would he have the physical strength to strangle Malloy?"

"If he had help," Jay said. "Maybe from a former baseball star who recently lost everything."

Mel gasped. "You think the Hargraves were working with Scottie Jensen?"

"And maybe others," Jay said.

"A conspiracy then?" Mel asked. "Malloy certainly made enough enemies. I wonder if the police have thought of this."

Jay shrugged. "I'm just glad I didn't have anything invested with him. Messy business."

Mel nodded in agreement.

Just then Poppy came tottering out of the restroom and looped her hand around Jay's elbow. She gave Mel a look that clearly said *mine*.

"Come on, let's go buy me something pretty," she said.

Jay smiled indulgently. "Of course, darling. We'll be right back."

"Take your time," Mel said. The cupcakes would be done in five minutes, but then they'd have to cool.

She saw Mr. and Mrs. Felix in the main part of the bakery. She knew they had been banking on Baxter Malloy's investment for their retirement. She wondered how they felt about him now.

"I love your bakery, Mel," Mrs. Felix said. She was examining one of the cupcake potholders Mel sold on their rack of cupcake kitsch in the corner. "It has such charm."

"Thank you," she said. "Mr. Felix, I wanted to tell you how sorry I was to hear about Baxter Malloy's investment scam. I hope you'll be all right."

Mr. Felix gazed at her with such sad eyes that Mel instantly regretted saying anything.

"I can only hope he is burning in the fires of hell," he said. His eyes may have been sad, but his voice was so full of anger it shook, as if he barely had a handle on it.

"Let's not talk about this," Mrs. Felix said. "You'll just get all worked up again, and the doctor told you to be careful about your stress level. You can't afford another heart attack."

Now Mel really felt bad. She was only asking because she was worried about her mother, and here she was causing someone else untold grief.

"I'm sorry," she said. "I shouldn't have said anything."

"Don't think on it," Mrs. Felix said. "It's perfectly reasonable for you to worry about us. How is your mother by the way? Was it terrible for her?"

"Yeah, pretty terrible," Mel said.

"I'm sorry for her," Mr. Felix said. "But I'm not sorry he's dead, the rat bastard."

Mel met his gaze, and the banked anger within his eyes flared to life, and for an instant she could almost picture Mr. Felix causing Baxter Malloy harm — severe harm.

The oven timer went off, and Mel found herself quite happy to excuse herself to head back to the kitchen. Angie bounced back in through the back door while Mel was pulling out the cupcakes. She placed them on the center of the table to cool, while Angie rambled on and on about Roach.

Mel felt her mind wander, and she let it. It was better than hearing the sordid details of someone else's really cool love life, since her own had been downgraded to one step above coed napping on mats in preschool.

"And then I lit my hair on fire and ran around the room naked," Angie said.

"Huh . . . what?" Mel asked. She'd heard the words *fire* and *naked* and figured she'd better tune back in.

"You're not listening," Angie said.

"Sorry," Mel admitted. "It's this murder. I can't stop thinking about how someone murdered Malloy just feet from my mother but didn't harm her. I'm grateful, but I can't help worrying . . ."

"That whoever it is might change their mind and come after her?" Angie asked.

"Yeah."

"Well, I know how you feel, I'm dating one of the chief suspects," Angie said. She fretted her lower lip between her teeth. "I hate that the tabloids keep running stories about Roach. I'd really like to see them find the real killer."

Mel thought Roach could very well be the killer, but she refrained from saying anything that might make Angie angry with her. She needed to keep Angie close so she could keep an eye on her.

"I was talking to Jay, and he said that there are so many people who lost so much, he thinks there's more than one person involved in the murder," she said.

"So they all took turns twisting the stocking around Malloy's neck?" Angie asked. "Somehow I think your mother would have noticed a crowd outside her cabana."

"Maybe it was just a group that did the planning," Mel said.

"But why?" Angie asked. "That wouldn't get their money back."

"Unless they were trying to get Baxter to give it back," Mel said.

"And they went too far." Angie shuddered. "I don't like this. Give me a crime of passion over a coldly plotted murder any day."

"I wonder what the Hargraves are doing tonight?" Mel asked.

"You're not going over there."

"Why not?" Mel asked. "I'll pretend to be making a cupcake delivery and get the wrong house."

"Mel, these people are billionaires," Angie said. "They have vicious guard dogs and security personnel. Shoot, they probably have land mines to keep the riffraff — which would be you — out."

"They're not billionaires anymore," Mel said. "I'm going."

"Fine, but you're not going alone. I'm coming with you," Angie said. When Mel began to protest, she raised her hand. "No arguing."

Mel closed her mouth as her class returned, and she plastered on her encouraging teacher's smile. Meanwhile she mentally reviewed what sort of cupcake would get her past a killer guard dog. Somehow, carrot cake did not seem likely. Sadly, she didn't have any bacon-flavored ones.

"So, what are you going to say?" Angie asked as they pulled up outside a large stone mansion perched on the side of Camelback Mountain.

"I'm going to say I have a delivery," she said. "And then I'm going to bluff."

"Fall back and punt," Angie said. "Nice. Remember, if you get into trouble, I'll be listening."

Angie pulled back out onto the road and then took a sharp right into the narrow driveway in front of the mansion. There was a steep drop to the right, and Mel saw Angie's grip on the steering wheel tighten.

"What kind of an idiot builds an eleven-thousand-square-foot house on the side of a damn mountain?" she griped. "I mean, really, how much space do two people need?"

She parked in front of a five-car garage. Mel called her cell phone, and Angie answered. Their plan was to keep their cell phones on so Angie could listen in and be ready if Mel needed backup. At least the mountain wouldn't cut off their reception given that they were on top of it. Mel took a box of cupcakes out of the back seat and strode towards the three-story glass-and-concrete fortress.

For the first time, she questioned the wisdom of her plan. Mercifully, there were no guard dogs in sight. In fact, there was no one in sight. The house seemed awfully dark, and she wondered if the Hargraves were out. Nuts. She should have called first.

She climbed three wide steps onto a large terrace. Large potted cacti stood like sentries on either side. Feeling edgy, she checked her phone.

"You there, Ange?"

"Roger."

"We have to learn some better lingo. Shouldn't there be a code four or something?"

"Quit stalling."

Mel put the phone back in the front pocket of her bag. She crossed the terrace and paused in front of the massive wooden doors. She didn't see a doorbell, so she used the enormous iron door knocker that hung on the middle of the right door. It banged so hard against its base that Mel jumped.

"That's some door knocker," she said out loud for Angie's benefit.

She waited. No one answered. She banged again. Still no answer.

She stepped back and tried to peer into

207

the windows above. There was no light, no movement.

She took her phone out of her bag. "I think this is a bust, Angie. No one's home."

"What —" Angie began but was cut off by a deep grinding noise.

Mel glanced up to see if it was coming from the house, but no. It was coming from where Angie was parked.

Mel's phone suddenly squawked with profanity, and she heard a squeal of tires as Angie's car came shooting in reverse from in front of the garage right towards the edge of the mountain.

SIXTEEN

A huge mover's truck barreled out of the garage. The cab of the truck was caught in the headlights of Angie's car and Mel could see that an old lady with gray hair was driving, a younger man was in the middle, and sitting shotgun was an old man. Mel at once recognized the two oldsters as the Hargraves.

She raced to the edge of the terrace, half-afraid the old lady was going to ram Angie down the side of the mountain. But Mrs. Hargrave turned the wheel hard to the right and missed Angie by a breath. Then she rolled down her window and yelled, "Take the house, you parasites, but you'll never take us alive!"

Mr. Hargrave shot them a rude hand gesture as the moving truck rumbled down the drive and away.

Angie drove her car slowly forward. She parked it, got out, and sat on the ground.

Mel rushed over and handed her a Cherry Bomb Cupcake.

"Thanks," Angie said. Her fingers were shaking, but she managed to peel the paper off and take a bite. "I thought that crazy old bat was going to send me to the big bakery beyond."

Mel sat down beside her. She took another cupcake out of the box, a Tinkerbell, and bit into it.

"I think my heart stopped," she said. "If I could mainline this frosting, I think I would."

"Uh-huh," Angie said. She reached into the box for another. She downed an Espresso-Shot Cupcake and then took a deep breath. Mel reached for a Death by Chocolate, and only after she finished it did she feel a little better. At least her heart had resumed beating.

"So, what do we do now?" Angie asked.

Mel shrugged. "It doesn't look good that the Hargraves have flown the coop. I think Jay was right. I think they were in on some-thing."

"But it sounded like they were running more from the bank than the law," Angie said. "I mean, you flip off a bill collector; you do not flip off the law."

"But I came with cupcakes," Mel protested. "Even if I was a bill collector, that was unduly harsh. Not to mention almost running you down."

"True," Angie said. "I repeat, what do we do now?"

"We need to find out where they are going, and who the man in the truck with them was," Mel said.

"Hired muscle?"

"Maybe," Mel said. "We're here. Should we check the house?"

"You think they left us a note telling us where to find them?" Angie asked. "Gee, how thoughtful."

"Sarcasm does not become you." Mel stood and brushed off the seat of her pants. Angie did the same.

"Really? I thought it was my best feature."

Mel put the box on the roof of the car, and they walked up to the open garage door. It was dark, and Mel felt along the wall for a light switch. With a snap, light flooded the multiple-bay garage. It was barren.

Angie crossed the room, her footsteps echoing on the hard concrete. A short staircase led up to a door, which was ajar. The Hargraves had left in such a hurry, they hadn't even bothered to close the door behind them.

"Hello?" Angie called. Mel frowned at her,

and she shrugged. "Just being polite."

They entered through a back hallway, which split into a large kitchen and living area. Mel fumbled along the way until she found another light switch. Recessed lighting in the cathedral ceiling cast a celestial glow down the walls.

"Is it just me, or are you feeling the need to genuflect?" Angie asked.

"Shh," Mel said. But she had to agree. She was half expecting to find a pulpit.

"Well, now we know why they needed the muscle," Angie said. "This place has been stripped."

She pointed over her shoulder with her thumb, and Mel looked over the wide granite counter to the collection of gaping holes in the wall. It was easy to see where the appliances once stood.

"Wow," she said. "I wonder if the whole house is like this."

"Let's check," Angie said. "I'll take upstairs."

She crossed the marble floor to the wide, winding staircase, flipping on lights as she went.

Mel toured the vacant rooms on the first floor. A bedroom, three bathrooms, an office, a formal dining room, and the outside patio, all completely bare. Every fancy fixture had been removed, even the toilet paper holders.

" 'And the one speck of food that he left in the house was a crumb that was even too small for a mouse.' " Angie's head appeared over the balcony railing above.

"How the Grinch Stole Christmas," Mel said, identifying the quote. "He struck down here, too."

Angie bounced down the stairs. "This is some crib."

Mel studied her. "Are you going to keep talking like you're on an MTV reality show?"

"What do you mean?" Angie blinked.

"Forget it," Mel said. Angie had put up with her through a gazillion bad boyfriends and crash diets over the years; surely Mel could put up with her during her rock-and-roll romance. "Let's go."

As they wandered out into the chilly desert evening, Mel was struck by the stunning view. The city lights rolled out in a twinkling carpet below a dusty lavender sky, meeting at the horizon in a ridge of deep purple mountains.

Nestled onto plateaus on the mountain sat other mansions, some lit, some not. The amount of money it would require to be one of these residents was not a number Mel could wrap her brain around. Luckily, she knew someone who could.

She pulled out her phone and called Tate.

"Hi, Mel," he answered on the second ring.

" 'For some players, luck itself is an art,' " she said.

The Color of Money," Tate replied. "Nice. Where are you?"

"On a mountain with Angie," she said.

"What, she doesn't have a hot date tonight?" he asked.

Mel sighed. How long exactly was it going to take Tate to figure out his feelings for Angie? For one of the country's top investment analysts, he was as dumb as a brick in matters of the heart.

"Moving on," she said. "I need a favor."

"Anything," he said, which was why she loved him.

"Baxter Malloy was dating a woman named Elle Simpson, a big, bold blonde type. I need to know anything you can find out about her."

"All right," Tate said. "What makes you think I can find anything out?"

"You have more access to the hoi polloi gossip than I do, and I think she's known for travelling in circles with rich men."

"A gold digger?"

"Precisely."

"On it," he said. "Anything else?"

"Yeah, do you know the Hargraves?"

"Only by reputation," he said. "They lost billions to Malloy."

"Can you find out if they have any children or other young relatives, say, a male in his early to mid-twenties."

"Why?"

"Just curious."

"Uh-huh, I get the feeling you're not telling me something," he said. Mel was silent. "Fine, be that way. I'll call you back when I have something."

Tate never called. Instead, he blew in through the front door of the bakery the next morning like a small tornado.

"You owe me," he said to Mel.

She raised her eyebrows in surprise.

"Where's Angie?"

"Not here yet," Mel said.

Tate checked his watch.

"But it's —" he began, but Mel interrupted him.

"I'm aware of the time."

"I keep telling her to fire that girl," Marty said. He was refilling the napkin holders in the booths.

"New employee?" Tate asked.

"A temp," Mel said.

Tate shook his head. "Okay, I had to have my mother call my aunt Penelope, who called her friend Beverly, who no one can stand."

Mel remembered the silver-haired lady at the museum luncheon who had not been fond of Elle. She'd bet her body weight in sprinkles that it was the same one.

"And?" she prompted him.

"Well, you were right. Elle Simpson is quite the money magnet. Before Baxter, she was shacked up with a major-league baseball star, a TV producer, and a fast-food franchise owner. Before that she was a B-movie actress who didn't get much further than the cutting-room floor."

"So, she's been around?" Mel asked.

"And how," Tate agreed. "She likes them old, and she likes them loaded, so Baxter was perfect for her."

"Except he really wasn't that well off," Mel said. "He was a scam artist."

"Sounds like a perfect match to me," Tate said.

"Except that if he was bankrolling her and then dumped her to find a wealthy woman to bail him out, Elle might have been a teeny bit upset."

"Enough to murder him?"

"I don't know," Mel said. "How about the

Hargraves?"

"They do have a nephew," Tate said. "Word has it he was kicked out of Yale, Cornell, Harvard, and Princeton."

"Impressive," Mel said.

"Apparently, he has an utter lack of social skills. He's twenty-eight, still lives with the Hargraves, and has never held a job in his life."

"I think I must have dated him," Mel joked.

"So, why do you need to know about these people?"

"They're the best suspects I've got for Malloy's murder," she said.

"Not the best," Tate argued. "That would be Roach."

Mel saw a spot on the counter and wiped it with the corner of her apron.

"You can't keep avoiding the obvious," he said. "He is the best suspect."

"Then why haven't the police charged him?" Mel asked.

"Because he's a rock star," Tate said. His voice was scathing, leaving no doubt in Mel's mind how he felt about Roach.

"All right, letting go of that for the moment, Angie and I went to the Hargraves' last night," Mel said.

"What?" Tate smacked his hand down on

the counter. "Are you crazy?"

Before he could continue his diatribe, Mel held up her hand and told him all about the previous evening. He listened intently and only grunted once or twice.

"So, I think we need to follow up and find out more about the Hargraves and Elle Simpson."

"How do you plan to do that?" Tate asked.

Mel tipped her head and looked him over. "You're probably too young for her. We need someone older, who can get close to her and find out what she knows."

"You need a rich geezer," Tate said.

They both turned to look at Marty.

"Don't look at me. The last time I went along with one of your brainiac ideas, I ended up in a Dumpster," he said.

"This time you'd have a babe on your arm," Mel said.

"Who'd have a babe?" Angie asked as she pushed through the kitchen door into the bakery.

"Where have you been?" Tate asked. He looked like an indignant mother waiting up past curfew.

"Breakfast," she said.

"At noon?" he sounded outraged.

"Is he for real?" Angie asked Mel.

"As a tick on a hound dog," Mel said.

"If you must know, the medical examiner has released Baxter Malloy's body. I was helping Roach work out the details of his funeral."

"Oh," Tate said. He looked away, obviously unwilling to acknowledge what a butt he was being.

Angie rolled her eyes at Mel. "He's managing. Thanks for asking."

"If he's the killer, I'm sure he is managing," Tate said. "Managing to cover up his crime."

"What are you talking about? He's not the killer," Angie said.

"You can't know that," Tate said. He turned to Mel. "Tell her."

"I . . ." Mel trailed off awkwardly.

"Tell me what?" Angie asked, glancing between the two of them.

"He lied," Tate said.

"Who lied?" Angie asked.

"Roach lied," Mel said.

SEVENTEEN

"Lied about what?" Angie asked.

"He told us the first day we met him that he was at rehearsal when his father was killed, but Carl and Jimbo told me that the band hasn't been practicing," Mel said. "I'm sorry, Angie, but it doesn't look good that he lied."

Angie stepped back from them and crossed her arms over her chest. Her lips were compressed as if holding back harsh words. Mel felt dread twist her insides. She didn't want to hurt Angie, but Tate was right. It was time to tell her the truth.

"Why didn't you say anything before?" Angie asked.

Mel shrugged. "You've been so happy. I didn't want to ruin it for you, and even if he did kill his father, I didn't see why he'd want to harm you. I've seen the way he looks at you. He's smitten."

"So you said nothing, even though I might

be dating a murderer?"

"My point exactly," Tate said. "I knew we should have told you sooner."

"You're the best!" Angie cried, threw her arms around Mel's neck, and hugged her close. "If you were dating a murderer, I wouldn't try to wreck it for you either."

"You're all crazy, you know that?" Marty said. "Plum crazy."

Mel hugged Angie back. She was so relieved. Angie knew the truth and she wasn't mad at her. Whew.

"What about me?" Tate asked. "Don't I get a hug?"

Angie stepped back and glowered at him. "After sending the brothers after me?"

Tate stepped back. Angie stepped forward.

"What makes you think I had anything to do with that?" he asked. He took another step back. "You know how overprotective they are."

"Oh, please. Do you have any idea how embarrassing it is to have your older brothers just appear at the bowling alley, at the movies, and at every meal you eat when you're trying to have a date?" she asked, taking another step forward. "Don't deny it. Every incident has had Tate Harper's sticky little fingers all over it."

"I don't think . . ."

"No, you don't," she agreed.

He took two quick steps back, and she pursued.

"Why aren't you mad at Mel?" he asked. "She's the one who snooped at the concert."

"Yes, but she wants me to be happy, and you don't," Angie snapped.

Tate's back was against the front door now. He looked to Mel for help, but she had none to offer. He was going to have to fess up to his real feelings or suffer Angie's wrath.

"I want you to be happy," he said. "Just not with . . ."

The door was abruptly yanked open by a customer, and Tate went sprawling onto the sidewalk.

Angie pulled the customer in by the elbow, then slammed and locked the door. She wiped her hands together as if she'd just taken out the trash, then turned her most charming smile on the middle-aged woman before her.

"Hi. Welcome to Fairy Tale Cupcakes. What can I get for you?"

Mel and Marty exchanged alarmed looks. Angry Angie was always a sight to behold. Tate bounced up off the walk and knocked on the door. Angie pulled the mini-blinds shut and led the woman over to the counter, her smile still in place.

Mel hurried to the door and unlocked it. She poked her head out and said, "You'd better go. I'll call you later."

"Why is she so mad at me?" Tate asked. "I'm just looking out for her."

"Why? Tate, ask *yourself* why."

"I'm asking you why," he said. He frowned. "How am I supposed to know why she's so mad at me?"

Mel heaved an impatient sigh. "Tate, focus. Ask yourself why you feel the need to look out for her at all."

"Because she's my fr—" he began, but Mel cut him off.

"No! Ask yourself. I don't want to hear it."

She turned just as the middle-aged woman was leaving with a big box in her hands. Mel held open the door and let it swing shut behind her.

"You can't lock Tate out," she said to Angie. "It's bad for business, plus he's our partner."

Angie grumbled, but she didn't lock the door again.

"Now what are you going to do about Roach?" Mel asked.

"What do you mean?" Angie asked.

"You have to find out where he was when

his father was murdered," Mel said. "I didn't want to tell you but, now that you know, you have to follow up."

"No, I don't," Angie said.

"Ange!" Mel wailed. "I get that you like him. I do. But you can't ignore the facts."

"I'm not," Angie said. She met Mel's gaze and held it. "I know where he was when his father was killed. He told me on our first date."

"And?" Mel asked.

"And I promised I wouldn't tell anyone," she said.

"I'm not anyone," Mel said, feeling a bit miffed.

"I know, but I promised," Angie said. "Trust me when I tell you that I know him, and I know he's innocent."

"You've only known him for a few days," Mel said.

"Sometimes that's all it takes," Angie said.

"He'd better have one heck of an alibi," Marty said.

Angie spun around to face him. She tipped her head as she studied him. "Are you working here now?"

"Someone had to fill in for you," he said. "Miss Always Late and Never Calls."

"He's a temp," Mel said. "Believe it or not, he has a way with our older female clientele."

"Oh, I believe it," Angie said. Marty stuck his tongue out at her. "But if you must know, yes, Roach has an alibi, a good one."

Mel didn't push it. She'd have to trust that if the police hadn't arrested him yet, then his alibi was legit. She just hoped Angie knew what she was doing.

"Okay then, I'm back where I started," Mel said. "I think Elle Simpson had motive and opportunity, and I think we need to find out more about her."

"This is the woman Baxter was two-timing with your mother?" Angie asked.

"Yes, and the day I went shopping with Mom for her dress, I ran into her twice. I think she was tailing my mother," Mel said.

"So, she was checking out the competition," Angie said.

"Yep, and given the fact that Baxter met my mother bidding at the car auction, I'm certain he thought she was a wealthy widow, who he planned to scam into investing in his crazy money schemes."

"No wonder Roach didn't talk to him," Angie said. "What a dirtbag."

"The question is, was Elle mad enough to kill him?"

"How can we find out?"

"We need someone to get close to her,"

Mel said. She glanced back at Marty. "Someone older and charming, who reeks of money and good breeding."

"Oh, no you don't. I still have a crick in my back from the Dumpster," he said.

"Come on, Marty," Angie cajoled. She threw an arm around his shoulders. "Do me a solid, and I'll give you ten free chances to win the raffle."

"Ten?"

"Did I say ten? Make that fifteen."

"Oh, all right," he said. "But I had better win."

Mel glanced over at the raffle box. She hadn't even been paying attention to the entries.

"It's almost full," Marty said.

"Nice to know the contest is working," Angie said. "Now how are we going to get Marty here suavified?"

"Suavified?" Mel asked.

"Like it? I just made it up." Angie beamed.

"I'm thinking we need Mean Christine."

"Oh." Angie pursed her lips. She'd had one waxing episode with Mean Christine that she had not quite gotten over. It was a bikini wax gone Brazilian when Mean Christine got carried away and didn't wax within the lines.

"I know it's drastic," Mel said. "But we're

under a time crunch, and she's the best in the biz. She'll have Marty looking snappier than Prince Charles."

"I think we can set the bar a little higher," Angie said. "Come on, let's go."

"Who is Mean Christine?" Marty asked. "I don't like this. What are you two planning? Is this going to hurt?"

"Only if you snivel," Angie said. "Christine does not respond well to whiners."

When Marty looked like he was going to dig his heels in, Angie and Mel each caught him by an elbow and led him out the door.

Mel locked the bakery up behind them, and they strode down the sidewalk to the salon around the corner on Brown Avenue. A neon sign hung over the door. In swirling script it spelled CHRISTINE'S; no one actually called her Mean Christine to her face.

A redhead wearing a turquoise wraparound smock sat at the front desk. Her hair was shoulder length with severely cut, straight bangs. She wore bright red lipstick and gold hoops in her ears. A brunette wearing the same smock, earrings, and lipstick sat beside her. Christine liked to have her employees look exactly like her, so they all had the same haircut and wore the same colors, right down to their accessories.

Mel tried to imagine Angie and herself

doing that at the bakery. A snort escaped her, and she felt Angie shoot her a quick glance. Mel could tell by the smile on her face that she'd been thinking the same thing.

"May I help you?" the redhead asked.

"We have an emergency," Mel said. "We need Marty turned into a metrosexual asap."

"What?" Marty started fighting their hold. "You are not touching my privates. I am a man, and I'm staying that way!"

"Marty, chillax!" Angie said. "A metrosexual is just a guy who gets his hair cut by a professional instead of wearing a hair hat."

"Oh," Marty settled down. "Why didn't you just say that?"

The two women behind the counter looked Marty over, from his worn orthopedics and baggy cardigan to the gray tufts on his head.

"Call Christine," the brunette said. "This is going to require more skill than we have combined."

A short while later, Christine appeared. She was tall and thin, with bluntly cut black hair. Instead of the turquoise smock, she wore a leopard print. She did have the same red lipstick and hoop earrings, however.

"What's the ruckus about?" she asked as

she came down the stairs from the back room.

"Emergency," Mel said. "This is Marty, and he needs, well, the works."

She glanced at Marty, who looked struck dumb at the sight of Christine. Mel couldn't blame him. Christine was one of those people who owned any room she walked into. With dark brown eyes that were almost black, she seemed to see everything all at once with a laser-like scrutiny that made the recipient of her gaze aware of every hair that was out of place, every pore that was clogged, and every jagged fingernail.

Christine turned to her two assistants. "Take Marty to one of our changing rooms and have him put on a robe."

Marty gave Mel and Angie a bug-eyed look while he was led off by the two young lovelies.

"This is going to cost you," Christine said.

Mel sighed. She'd figured. "How much?"

"More than you can afford," Christine said. "However, you're in luck. I need a favor."

"I'm listening."

"Wedding for three hundred people," Christine said. "Four different kinds of cupcakes in a tier with a larger cake on top for cutting. It's for my niece."

"When?" Mel asked.

"April."

"Have her stop in to pick flavors and colors, and consider it done," Mel said.

Christine's lips twitched at the corners, which was the closest she ever came to a smile. One of her assistants reappeared with a plastic bag. She handed it to Christine, who handed it to Mel.

"Those are his things," she said. "When you pick him up, have new clothes for him. I can't let my work be buried behind a polyester sweater and plastic shoes."

"Will do," Mel said.

She and Angie turned and left. When they stepped outside, Angie let out a sigh of relief.

"Better him than me," she said.

"Still not over it?" Mel asked.

"A few more therapy sessions, and then we'll see," Angie said. "Poor Marty. I feel like I just left my puppy at the groomer's for his first haircut."

"Don't worry about Marty," Mel said. "He's a scrappy little fellow. If anyone can give Christine a run for her wax pot, it's him."

EIGHTEEN

"We're going to need clothes," Angie said.

"Yes, and they're going to have to be expensive," Mel agreed.

"Now what man do we know with a killer wardrobe?"

"Tate," they said together.

"Should we call him?" Angie asked.

"We don't want to bother him at work," Mel said. "Besides, we just need a suit or two. Then we'll need to have them tailored a bit."

"I have my key to his place," Angie said.

"Okay, you go get the clothes, and I'll see if I can get someone to do the quick fix."

"On my way," Angie said.

They parted in front of the bakery. Mel opened the door and hurried back inside.

She got no farther than the kitchen when her cell phone started ringing.

"Hello," she answered.

"Melanie, where have you been?" Joyce

asked. "I've been calling the shop, but there was no answer. I thought there may have been a fire or a flood or worse."

"I had to run an errand," Mel said.

"Shouldn't someone always be at the shop?" Joyce asked. "You could lose business that way, and in this economy, you can't expect Tate or dear Joe to bail you out."

"I wouldn't expect them to," Mel said. She tried not to bristle at the lecture. "Mom, don't worry. The business is fine. Now, what's up?"

"I'm just . . . I don't know. Since Charlie and Nancy and the boys left, it's so quiet here. I suppose I'm being silly, but something feels wrong," she said. "And then Detective Martinez stopped by . . ."

"Back up," Mel said. "Who stopped by?"

"Detective Martinez," her mother answered.

The door to the bakery opened, and two ladies walked in. Mel smiled at them and signaled that she'd be just a minute.

"What did he want?" Mel asked.

"He seems very concerned that I didn't see anyone that night," Joyce said. "I tried to explain that I was in the cabana changing, but he thinks I should have heard a splash when Baxter fell in or was

232

pushed . . .”

Mel could feel her teeth clench. She didn't like that Martinez was asking her mother questions again. She didn't like that he was insinuating that Joyce should have heard something.

"Mom, have you called Uncle Stan?" she asked.

"No, I was going to wait until after I talked to you," she said. "I don't want to bother him."

"It's no bother," Mel said. "He'd want to know."

"Well, if you think that's best," Joyce said.

"I do."

The two ladies were now standing in front of the counter waiting to place their orders.

"I have to go, Mom, but I'll call you later," she said. "Call your friend Ginny and go out to lunch. I don't want you to brood about this. It's going to be fine."

"That's a good idea," Joyce said. "I'll talk to you later."

Mel hung up the phone, wishing for the first time that her mother had gotten a look at the killer. At least then she'd be able to tell the police something that would get them to leave her alone. Of course, then she might be in danger from the killer herself. It was a sobering thought.

Mel plastered on a smile and served the two ladies their cupcakes. It was a warm day for February, so the two women were eating them outside at the small café tables in front of the shop. Normally, Mel was delighted to have people eat outside because she felt it drew attention to the shop, but today she just wanted to close up and race over to her mother's and give her a bracing hug.

What if Martinez didn't find the real killer and decided to arrest Joyce? Mel didn't want to have her boyfriend prosecuting her mother for a crime she didn't commit. Truly, that would be the stuff of nightmares.

She forced herself to stop thinking about it and placed a phone call to an acquaintance who owed her a favor. Within five minutes she had what she wanted and hung up with a grin.

Her phone rang again and, thinking it was the acquaintance calling to back out, she snatched up the receiver.

"Fairy Tale Cupcakes, how can I help you?"

"Ear-hair surcharge," a muffled voice said.

"What?" she asked.

"Hang on," the muffled voice said. There was a rustling noise as if the phone was being moved around.

"There is going to be an ear-hair surcharge." This time Mel could tell it was Christine. "I just wanted to let you know in advance. Seriously, I have carpets with less fur."

"Yowch!" A voice Mel feared was Marty's yipped in the background.

"Is he okay?" she asked, but Christine had already hung up.

The front door to the bakery opened and in strode Angie with two suits slung over her arm. "I took an Armani and a Prada. Tate must have fifty pounds on Marty, do you think we can tailor them?"

"We can't, but Alma Rodriguez can," Mel said.

"The scary-looking design girl who used to work for Tate's late fiancée?" Angie asked.

"That's the one," Mel said.

"How are you going to get her to do that?"

"She owes me," Mel said.

As if their conversation had beckoned her, Alma Rodriguez pulled open the door and entered the bakery.

Both Mel and Angie stared. They hadn't seen Alma in several months, and what a transformation she had made from a black-clad goth girl to a stunner in narrow heels and an olive green tailored suit that hugged and flared in all the right places. Whereas before she had resembled a petulant teen, now she exuded a mature confidence that awed and intimidated.

"What?" Alma snapped, staring at the two of them.

"Well, at least you still have your charm," Mel said.

A small smile curved Alma's lips. "Sorry, old habits die hard."

"You look amazing," Angie said.

Alma did a small pirouette. "Terry, my boss, sort of insisted. He was right. You can't be a jet set designer and look like you've got an algebra exam in the morning."

"Thanks for agreeing to help us out," Mel said.

"I had a choice? I know I owe you one — a big one," Alma said. "It's the least I can do. Where is the old guy?"

Mel handed over Tate's suits and said, "He's getting cleaned up over at Mean Christine's salon."

Alma cringed. "How old is he?"

"Somewhere in his seventies," Mel said.

"I hope he's spry," Alma said. "A day with Christine could kill a weakling."

"Don't I know it," Angie said.

They exchanged a look of understanding, and Mel suspected Alma had suffered a similar trauma at Christine's.

"I'll just take these over there and get some measurements. If I get my staff on it right away, we can probably have these altered in a couple of hours."

"Perfect," Mel said. "Thanks, Alma."

"And then we're square?" Alma asked.

"Totally."

Alma nodded in satisfaction and left.

As the door shut, Angie looked at Mel and said, "Next step?"

"Phase two," Mel said. "We're going to need an introduction for Marty and Elle."

"Well, he can't show up at her house bearing cupcakes," Angie said. "What's your plan?"

"Tate and Aunt Penelope are going to have to set it up."

"He's not going to like this."

"He's not going to like his Prada and Armani being altered either," Mel said. "But it's for the greater good."

She called Tate. He answered on the third ring.

"Harper Investments, Tate Harper speaking," he said.

" 'If I didn't know you better, I'd swear you had some class,' " Mel said.

"The Sting!" Tate said, identifying the movie quote. "Good one. Are we watching that this week?"

"Or living it," Mel said. "Depending upon how you look at it."

"What's going on?" Tate asked. His voice was wary.

"I need to work out an introduction," Mel said. "Between Marty and Elle."

"Between . . . ? You have got to be kidding me," he said.

"Nope, very serious," Mel said. "Angie and I . . ."

"So, Angie is there, too?" he asked. "She's not off with her boyfriend again?"

Mel let out a sigh. "Focus, Tate. Can you call your aunt and get her to introduce Marty and Elle?"

"Oh, man," he groaned. "Can't I just climb Mount Everest and bring down some fresh snow for you? It'd be less painful."

"Sorry, no," Mel said.

"I'll see what I can do," he said. "Oh, I also have a lead on the Hargraves."

"Nice, what do you know?"

"Mrs. Hargrave has a cousin in town, and my mother heard from a woman at her country club that the Hargraves are staying with them."

"Did you get a name?"

"Yeah, hang on. I wrote it down." Mel heard Tate shuffle some papers. "Irene Bakerson."

Mel gasped. "Married to Dan?"

"Uh, yeah, that's the one," Tate said. "How did you —"

Mel interrupted. "I have to go."

"Just remember you owe me one," he said. "A big one."

Mel thought of his suits. "You have no idea," she said. "Later." She hung up before he could ask any questions.

"What's going on?" Angie asked. She'd been hovering near Mel through the whole conversation.

"You are not going to believe it," Mel said.

"Try me."

"The Hargraves are the cousins of our very own Bickersons."

"Get out!"

"I'm planning to. I'm going to go stake out their house and see what's what. Maybe they're all in it together," Mel said.

She lifted her apron off of her head and hung it on a hook by the kitchen door. Angie made to do the same, but Mel stopped her.

"I need you here to man the bakery and answer the phone in case Christine calls to tell us Marty is done."

"Oh, man," Angie whined.

Mel gave her a look. She didn't want to have to point out that people skills were not

239

Angie's gift. If Mel got caught, she could bluff. Angie would never be able to pull that off.

"Fine, but come straight back here, and I want a full report."

"Roger that."

Mel stopped by her office and looked up the Bickersons' address on their registration form. They were in the neighborhood, less than a mile away. Excellent.

She dashed out to her car and headed south on Scottsdale Road and east on Osborn. She was in an older neighborhood now. The houses were small, red-brick ranch houses with square windows.

She turned south and then east again, stopping at the end of the Bickersons' street. She didn't think they knew what type of car she drove so she decided to drive by their house. There was a car in the carport, but no sign of anyone out front. The vertical blinds were all shut.

She drove to the end of the street and decided to drive down the alley that ran behind the house to see what was visible in the backyard.

She counted off the houses as she lurched slowly down the dirt-packed alley. At the seventh house, she stopped her car, got out, and jogged two more houses down until she was at the Bickersons' residence.

She heard the sound of laughter, and she crouched low.

She couldn't recall ever having heard the Bickersons laugh before. Maybe she had the wrong house.

"Oh, Miriam. I need a warm-up," a voice called.

Mel glanced over the wall to see Dan and Irene sitting in lounge chairs by their pool. Dan was reading the newspaper, while Irene was thumbing through a magazine. They were wearing matching sweaters remarkably similar to the ones Mel had seen Lester and Miriam Hargrave wearing at the museum luncheon.

"Miriam, did you hear me?" Irene called out.

The back door burst open. Mel ducked low and pressed her eye to a gap in the back gate, through which she could just see the Bickersons.

"I heard you. In fact I'm sure the entire neighborhood heard you." Miriam Hargrave stomped out the back door, carrying a coffee pot. She dutifully refilled the mugs on the small table between Irene and Dan.

"I don't think I like your tone, Miriam," Irene said. "If you want to keep staying here with us, you'd best watch your attitude."

Miriam turned on her heel and grumbled as she stomped her way back to the house. When the door shut behind her, Irene leaned over and kissed Dan on the cheek.

"I've always wanted domestic staff," she said. "You're a genius, dear."

Dan lowered his newspaper and gave Irene a beaming smile. "Thank you, love. It's more than they deserve after they swindled you out of your inheritance. They're lucky we let them stay here at all. A little light labor will do them good."

Irene chortled.

"How's that fish pond coming, Harvey?" Dan called.

Mel moved so she could see in the direction he had shouted. The young man from the moving van was working in the corner of the yard. He was standing in a hole and was covered in sweat and streaks of dirt.

"It's coming," he snarled. He was clearly not enjoying the task he'd been given.

Irene and Dan seemed to find his annoyance funny as they clinked coffee cups and beamed at him. This seemed to make Harvey out-and-out mad, and he picked up his shovel and began to dig furiously. Irene and Dan shared a laugh at his ire and went back to their reading.

Mel eased away from the gate. Well, it

looked as if the Bickersons were finally getting along. Maybe uniting against a common enemy was all they needed to rekindle their romance.

If the Hargraves had taken Irene's inheritance and invested it with Malloy, they not only stole it but also lost it. She really couldn't fault the Bickersons for enjoying their revenge. It did make her wonder, though, how far Dan and Irene would go to get even.

She pulled out her cell phone and glanced at the time. Christine should be about done with Marty by now, and Angie would need support at the shop. Mel hurried back to her car, wondering if Detective Martinez knew about the Hargraves and if she was brave enough to tell him.

"Your lattes," the redhead said as she put a tray on the table in front of Mel and Angie.

Mel and Angie were sitting in Mean Christine's waiting room. The altered suits had been delivered by Alma, and Christine was in a back room with Marty, making sure they fit. Angie had "borrowed" a pair of Gucci loafers from her brother Tony, as he wore the same shoe size as Marty.

Mel sipped the froth off of her coffee, trying to channel her patience. She had filled

Angie in on what she'd discovered at the Bickersons', but neither of them knew what to do with the information.

They'd been waiting twenty minutes for Marty to appear, so Mel figured it had either gone horribly wrong and Christine was trying to do damage control, or it had gone amazingly well and she was milking her success for every ounce it was worth. Given all that Mel had riding on this transformation, she hoped it was the latter.

Finally a back door opened, and Christine strode out. Her blunt black hair was mussed, and her glasses were slightly askew, as if she'd spent a grueling afternoon pedaling uphill in the Tour de France.

She dropped into a seat beside Mel and said, "Behold."

And then a very dapper, older gentleman appeared. Mel squinted, trying to see the fusty old Marty underneath the veneer of urbanity in which he was now swathed.

His wispy hair had been cut short and made a fuller fringe around his dome, which had been polished to a high gloss. His skin looked pink and healthy and less wrinkled than the sallow paper sack it had once resembled.

Both Mel and Angie rose slowly to their feet. They walked around him with their mouths slightly agape.

"Marty, you're a stud," Angie declared.

His chest puffed out a bit, and Mel had to admit he looked like a million bucks. But there was something different about him, something that couldn't be gotten from mere exfoliation and tweezing.

"Marty, are you taller?" Mel asked. "And where are your glasses?"

Christine met his gaze and put a finger in front of her pursed lips. Marty nodded at her in silent understanding and said, "I don't know what you mean."

Nineteen

"How did she do it?" Mel asked as they returned to the bakery. Marty was walking ahead of them, and instead of his sidewalk-scuffing old-man shuffle he now had a jaunty spring in his step. "You can't just make someone taller."

"Maybe he's wearing lifts," Angie said. "Or maybe she stretched him out on a rack."

"Weird," Mel said.

"And not a little scary," Angie agreed.

Tate was waiting for them when they reached the bakery. He had on an apron and was packing a dozen cupcakes for a young mother holding a baby and pushing another in a stroller.

"Where have you been?" he asked, mostly to Angie.

"Getting Marty cleaned up," she said.

Tate did a double take at Marty, and his eyes widened. "Marty? Wow. You look twenty years younger."

"Thanks." Marty preened.

"Nice suit by the way," Tate said. "I have one just like it."

Mel and Angie both turned to coo at the baby in her mother's arms.

"I'll walk you out," Marty offered, carrying the box of cupcakes for the woman, who looked desperately grateful.

"So, how did it go with your aunt Penelope?" Mel asked.

"There's good news and bad news," Tate said.

"Bad first," Angie said. Mel nodded. Angie always wanted the bad first, and she agreed.

"Aunt Penelope will only help if you provide baby shower cupcakes for her niece, one hundred in pink and blue," he said.

"When?" Mel asked.

"March."

Angie and Mel looked at each other and nodded.

"Doable," Mel said.

"Good, because I already said okay. Now listen, I've got it all set up," he said. "My aunt Penelope is meeting Elle at the Biltmore tonight under the pretense of some fashion show for charity. Marty and I will need to be in the lobby at six-thirty. We'll have to work out our story on the ride over."

Marty reentered the bakery, adjusting his lapels before striking a pose beside the display case.

"That only gives us a half hour," Mel said. "Let's go."

She and Angie went to grab their purses, but Tate stopped them. "No, you two aren't coming."

"Of course we are," Mel said.

"No, this is just a meet and greet," Tate said. "You two lurking in the lobby will give us away. Besides, the last time you two went to check someone out, you nearly got run off a mountain."

"Not exactly the last time," Angie muttered, but Tate ignored her.

"But —" Mel began to argue, but Tate cut her off.

"No buts. I'll call when we have something to report. Besides, you can't keep closing the shop on a whim. It's bad for business."

"It's not a whim," Mel pouted. "It's vital to my mother's — and by extension *my* — sanity."

Tate ignored her. "Ready, Marty?"

"Absolutely." He gave Mel and Angie a smart salute and led the way out the door.

"I'll call when I have news," Tate said. The door banged shut behind him.

"I feel like we just got shut out," Angie said.

"I think we did."

"Well, that stinks."

"Agreed," Mel said. She didn't like the idea of Marty and Tate going off on their own. What if they blew it? This was her idea after all. She should be in charge.

"Come on," she said to Angie. "I'm sure we can blend in with the furniture, and they'll never know we're there."

"Sweet." Angie flipped the sign to CLOSED, and they hustled out the door, locking it behind them.

The Biltmore was a Phoenix landmark. Built in 1929 with the influence of Frank Lloyd Wright, its consulting architect, it was one of Mel's favorite places in the Valley of the Sun.

They hopped into Mel's Mini Cooper, followed Camelback Road into Phoenix, and turned north on 24th Street. Another right took them on the long, winding road towards the beautifully sculpted gray-stone building. The precast concrete blocks, called Biltmore Block, used to make the building were etched with a geometric pattern that was supposed to mimic the patterns found on a palm tree.

"I heard that the pool here was Marilyn

Monroe's favorite," Angie said.

"It is a spectacular pool," Mel agreed. "I read somewhere that Irving Berlin penned 'White Christmas' while sitting beside it."

"Can you imagine lounging in your bikini when Elvis strolled by?"

"I'd probably jump in to spare myself the embarrassment."

They parked in the guest lot and walked towards the main entrance. Just before they reached the door, Angie pulled Mel aside.

"We should probably find a side entrance," she said. "We might get spotted otherwise."

"Good thinking," Mel said.

They passed the main door and walked around the building to the lawn and terrace. It was lovely, with flowers bursting and fountains bubbling, a slice of paradise.

Mel crossed the lawn and followed the line of the building until she found the door that led into the back of the lobby.

Squared off chairs and tables, done in earth tones to match the stone interior, were scattered around the room. Here and there large pots and other symbols of Native American art accented table tops and walls.

It really was a lovely room. Mel had no time to ponder more than this, as Angie gripped her elbow and yanked her down low.

"There they are!" she cried. Sure enough, Marty and Tate were lounging in plump leather seats when two women entered the lobby. Mel recognized one as Elle and assumed the other was Tate's aunt Penelope.

The men rose and greeted the ladies. Tate took over the introductions. Marty bowed low over Elle's hand, and Mel could see her sizing him up from where they were watching.

Just then, an older lady entered the lobby. She crossed the room with all the finesse of a tank. Mel clutched Angie's arm in a panic.

"That's Beverly," she hissed. "She was at the luncheon. She may recognize Marty."

Angie groaned, and the two of them peered over the edge of the sofa to see what would happen. Pleasantries were exchanged. Beverly and Elle were perfectly icy to each other, and then Beverly rolled on.

She was headed straight for Mel and Angie. Mel tried not to draw any more attention to herself, but the shrewd old eyes saw her, and Beverly paused beside them as she pretended interest in a lush floral arrangement.

"Your waiter is setting his sights rather low," she said. "I'd warn him to watch his neck if I were you."

With that she sashayed off in the direction

of one of the banquet rooms.

"Oh my God," Angie whispered. "She recognized Marty. Do you think she'll tell?"

"No," Mel said. "I think that was a warning for Marty about Elle. It sounds like she thinks Elle murdered Baxter."

"We're getting warmer," Angie said.

They glanced back at the group. The ladies were walking towards them while the men headed for the door.

"We'd better go if we plan to beat them back to the bakery," Mel said.

They hustled out the side door and around the building to the parking lot. When they reached Mel's car, Tate and Marty were waiting for them.

"What's the matter?" Tate asked. "Did you think we couldn't handle it?"

"No, it's not that," Mel protested.

"Really? Then why are you here?"

"We felt left out," Angie said.

Tate glanced between them. "Seriously?"

"Yeah," they said together.

"So, how did it go?" Mel asked.

"I have a date with the fair Ms. Simpson for tomorrow evening," Marty said.

"She practically tattooed her number onto his palm," Tate said. "Marty was perfect. He really played up being a member of the New York elite looking to retire here."

"Nice." Angie beamed at Marty, and he grinned.

"Listen, we'd best not be seen together," Mel said. "Can't have you two associating with the riffraff."

She didn't mention Beverly spotting them. She didn't want to panic either of them unnecessarily. There'd be plenty of time for that on Marty's date with Elle.

Mel had so much to tell Joe. She hardly knew where to begin. But then, when he knocked on the door with Gerbera daisies in one hand and a take-out bag from De-Falco's Italian Deli in the other, she forgot about anything but him.

"How is the case going?" she asked as he shed his suit jacket and loosened his tie.

"Ugh," he said. "I believe in everyone's right to a fair trial, but we've got this guy dead to rights. We have his plate number, a witness who can identify him, and the purchase receipt for the gun he used, which ballistics has linked to the shootings. And still, his defense attorney is throwing up every roadblock he can."

"So, the system works?" Mel asked.

Joe pulled her close and kissed her. He pulled back and looked her in the eye.

"Have I told you how much the thought

of coming over here at the end of the day and being with you helps me get through the insanity?"

"Not lately," she said. "But I feel the same way."

She carried the daisies and the take-out bag into the kitchenette and started unloading their dinner. The daisies went into a clear glass vase, which Mel put in the middle of her small café table, where she and Joe sat on opposite sides. He had a manly meatball sub while she had the scrambled egg and pepperoni. It was divine.

They chatted some more about his case and a little about Angie and her new boyfriend. Mel found herself reluctant to mention Marty or his date with Elle. She had the feeling Joe wouldn't approve, and she didn't want to damage the one night where he actually seemed well rested.

Maybe tonight would finally be the night.

They cleared up together and then snuggled on the couch. As Joe went to kiss her again, Mel was sure that he was thinking the same thing she was, and it made her pulse pound in her ears.

The theme to *Gone with the Wind* chimed from her cell phone, which was sitting in its dock on the counter. They pulled apart and looked at it and then back at each other.

"You'd better check it," Joe said. "It might be Ange with boyfriend trouble." He sounded hopeful.

Mel hopped up and glanced at the ID. It was her mother.

"Hello," she answered. She mouthed *Mom* to Joe, and he nodded.

"Melanie," Joyce said. "I need you to come over."

"Now?" Mel asked. She hoped she didn't sound as reluctant as she felt.

"Yes. I'm sure it's nothing, but I just feel funny," she said.

"Are you sick?"

Mel glanced at Joe, who raised his eyebrows in concern.

"No, I just — okay, I have the heebie-jeebies," Joyce said. "I hate to bother you, but if you could just come over and reassure me that everything is okay."

Mel glanced at Joe again and saw their romantic evening pop like a soap bubble in the air. Still, this was her mother. The woman who had checked her closet for monsters every night from ages four to eight, and who had come running in the middle of the night with soothing whispers and warm hugs whenever Mel woke up from a bad dream and called for her. How could Mel not do the same for her now?

"Sure, Mom, I'll be right over," she said. She hung up and grimaced at Joe. "I'm sorry. Mom's jittery. I have to go over and sweep the house with her."

"That's all right. I'll come, too," he said. He leaned forward to get up, but Mel shook her head.

"If you come, we'll never get out of there. She loves you. She'll ply you with coffee and pie and ask you a million personal questions."

"What kind of pie?"

Mel smiled. "Trust me, it's better if I go alone. I'll be quick, and then we can salvage our evening."

"I like the sound of that." Joe gave her his patent-worthy slow grin.

Mel felt a little cross-eyed from the impact. "Me, too."

She grabbed her jacket and keys, gave Joe a quick peck, and ran out the door.

Joyce was waiting for her in front of the house. Mel gave her a quick, firm hug of reassurance.

"Okay, Mom, what's got you spooked?"

"Well, I was doing the dishes, and I just got the weirdest feeling that someone was watching me," she said.

"Watching you?" Mel asked. This sounded more serious than her mother had made out on the phone. "Did you call Uncle Stan?"

"I don't want to bother him," she said. "He's already done so much."

"Okay, well, let's go through the house together," Mel said. "And then you can rest easy."

They went from room to room, checking windows and doors. The house was clear. When they arrived back in the kitchen, Mel went out into the backyard with a flashlight and checked the back gate. It was secure. She was turning to head back to the house when she noticed a footprint in the mud. She shined the flashlight on it.

Judging by the size and width, it was a man's footprint. Given that her brother had just been here, it wasn't unreasonable to assume that he had taken the garbage out and left a footprint. The troubling thing was that this imprint wasn't from the sort of shoe her brother would wear, a sneaker or a work boot.

This print looked more like a man's dress shoe with a narrow toe and short heel. The footprint faced her mother's home, as if he'd come in through the gate to watch the house. Mel felt a shudder ripple through her. She didn't like this, not at all.

She hurried back to the house. While her mother was getting ready for bed, Mel called her Uncle Stan and told him what she'd found. He sounded equally disturbed. He also said he was off duty and would head over to check it out. They both agreed that they wouldn't mention it to Joyce, because it would only upset her.

Mel was just hanging up when her mother came back into the kitchen. "Was that dear Joe?"

"No, that was Uncle Stan," Mel said. "He's going to stop by on his way home and check on you."

"He doesn't need to do that," Joyce protested. Mel saw the slight ease in her shoulders, though, and knew that, despite her protestations, she felt better having Uncle Stan come by.

"So, where is dear Joe tonight?" Joyce asked.

Mel glanced at the clock. She'd been gone almost an hour. "Probably, he's asleep on my couch by now."

"What?" Joyce squawked. "Why didn't you tell me you were on a date?"

"It was just dinner," Mel said.

"Just dinner? From what your brother said, I gather that's all it ever is with you two."

"Charlie told you . . ." Mel couldn't finish. She was speechless. Joyce, however, was not.

"That you haven't done the mattress mambo yet?" Joyce asked. "Yeah, he told me."

Mel felt her face flame hotter than a blowtorch.

"I'm going to kill him."

"Your time would be better spent on your boyfriend," Joyce said. She tossed Mel's jacket and keys at her and pushed her towards the door.

"How does everyone know about my sex life?" Mel asked. "Is there a billboard on the freeway or something?"

"There doesn't need to be," Joyce said. "We all know you. If you were sleeping with the man, you wouldn't be so uptight and edgy."

"I'm not uptight and edgy."

Joyce gave her a flat stare. "Honey, you have been in love with Joe DeLaura since you were twelve years old."

Mel nodded. It was true.

Her mother patted her cheek and said, "I say this to you with great love: Get the lead out. That boy is not going to wait forever."

Before Mel could say another word, her mother pushed her through the door and shut it behind her. She heard the deadbolt click into place.

"Well, there you have it. My humiliation is complete," Mel muttered as she strode to her car, grateful for the feel of the cool night air against her hot skin.

TWENTY

Mel spent the entire ten-minute ride home psyching herself up. Tonight was going to be the night. She and Joe were going to leap forward to the next level in their relation-ship, and then everyone could stop talking about her sex life and get back to their own.

She opened the front door, and a snore greeted her. To his credit, Joe looked as if he'd tried his best to stay awake. He had the remote in his hand, the TV was still on, he was even upright — all except his head, which had flopped onto the back of the couch. Thus, the snoring.

Mel sighed. So, they would not be moving to a new level tonight. She wondered if she should take this personally, but then decided no. If she had the biggest baking event of her life happening, she would expect Joe to be patient and let her do what she needed to do. Surely, she could do the same for him.

She locked the door and headed to the

bathroom, where she got ready for bed. When she returned, she prepped the bed around Joe, and then tossed the covers over the two of them. He pulled her close and buried his nose in her hair.

She could feel his warm breath against her skin, and it lulled her to sleep.

"The pigeon has landed."

"What?" Mel asked into her phone.

"The pigeon has landed," Angie repeated.

"She means they're here," Tate said. He and Angie were sitting at a restaurant table while Mel lurked in the kitchen. They had her on speakerphone.

Mel had arranged for Marty to take Elle to Les Terrines, a French restaurant in the heart of Phoenix. The executive chef was a cooking-school friend of Mel's and was letting her linger in the kitchen. She didn't want Elle to catch sight of her and suspect anything.

The restaurant was packed, but Tate and Angie had snagged a table on one side of a short wall, and Mel had arranged for the hostess to seat Marty and Elle on the other side. Mel hoped their plan worked. If Marty could get Elle talking about Baxter, maybe she would say something that would incriminate her in his murder. No one had as good of a motive . . . well, except maybe Roach, which she suspected was why Angie was here.

Mel glanced through the glass window of the kitchen door and saw Angie and Tate across the restaurant. Their faces were warmly lit by the small glass votive candle between them.

Tate was hanging on Angie's every word. It struck Mel for the first time that they were a perfect couple. Angie's zest for life kept Tate from being a complete dork, and his rock-solid dependability gave her stability. They had always enjoyed the same things and shared the same irreverent sense of humor.

For months now, Mel had watched Angie staring at Tate with her heart in her eyes. Now the tables had turned, and it was Tate looking at Angie as if he had a million things to say and no idea how to go about it. It had to be killing him that, with the arrival of Roach, he may have lost his chance.

The hostess strode into view with Marty and Elle following. Marty looked dapper in Tate's altered dark blue Prada. Elle, meanwhile, glittered in a sequined halter dress that accentuated all of her assets. Marty was the perfect gentleman and held her chair for her. As he took his seat, Elle looked at him as if she were trying to count the bills in his wallet before he sat down.

Tate and Angie both stilled as if trying to listen to the conversation on the other side of the wall from them. Tate, not very subtly, dropped his napkin. When he bent to retrieve it, he passed his cell phone under the table next to the leg of Marty's chair. Mel watched as Marty bent over and scooped it up, slipping it into his breast pocket as if he were just adjusting the fold of his handkerchief. Very smooth.

"So, Martin," Elle began. "Tell me, how did you make your fortune?"

"A little of this and a little of that," he said. "I like diversity."

Mel felt herself get tense. Marty couldn't be too vague or she'd figure out he was conning her.

Elle looked at him with shrewd eyes. Marty must have realized it, too, because he added, "Mostly, I dabbled in real estate, properties in the Hamptons and Palm Beach."

"The East Coast?" Elle's eyes lit up.

Mel got the feeling she was furnishing a beach house in her mind.

"Have you been there?" he asked.

"Not as much as I'd like," she said with a coquettish smile. Mel felt like gagging. Did that really work on a guy? She was going to have to ask Joe later.

"I'd love to show it to you," Marty said. He was channeling some serious suave here. "There is no other place for shopping like Manhattan, unless of course you're on the continent, in Paris or Milan."

Elle looked as if she might swoon.

Mel glanced at Angie and Tate's table to see if they were getting all of this. Judging by the sour look on Angie's face, they were.

Tate leaned over the table and said something to Angie, and her expression darkened into a tight-lipped, biting-back-her-anger glower, of which Mel was happy to note she had never been on the receiving end. But why was she furious with Tate?

Oh, no. Was Tate using their stakeout time to push his personal agenda of getting Angie to break up with Roach? Ack. This was terrible.

Mel glanced around the kitchen. She needed someone to run interference. Immediately! The kitchen staff was humming. She considered sending Monique, her cooking-school pal, out to their table, but she was having troubles of her own, as she was chewing out her sous-chef for plating a dish too early.

Mel would have gone out there herself,

but she couldn't risk being spotted. She wondered if she could peg Tate with a dinner roll from ten yards.

"Change of subject, please."

Mel heard Angie's voice on her cell phone. She couldn't hear Marty and Elle over Tate and Angie.

"No, you need to listen to me," Tate said. His voice was firm. He was trying to use his corporate muckety-muck voice on Angie. Mel could have told him that was a bad plan if he had bothered to ask her before he decided this was a good time to make Angie mad.

"No, I don't," Angie argued.

Mel peered through the small glass window in the swinging kitchen door. She stared at her friends, who were completely oblivious to the holes she was trying to burn into their skulls with the intensity of her gaze.

She tried to find their waiter. Someone needed to interrupt what was going to escalate into ugly any minute.

"You're being fatheaded about this whole thing, Ange," Tate said. "And you know it."

"Fatheaded?" Angie looked at him as if she might do him an injury with her butter knife.

"You can't seriously think that you're in

266

love with a rock-and-roll drummer whose stage name is Roach!"

"I can't?" Angie asked. "Watch me!"

Mel pushed halfway out the door. The hostess! She could send the hostess over. Mel crept out the kitchen door. She snatched a burgundy leather wine list and held it up to cover her face.

"Well, it looks like we got front row seats for the show," Marty joked. Elle laughed.

Marty spun around and gave Mel a desperate look. She nodded vigorously over the menu at him.

"Angie, you can do so much better than him," Tate said.

"Why would I want to?" Angie asked. Her voice was deceptively quiet, and if Tate had a brain in his head, he would have picked up on the danger and run.

Mel knew she was never going to make it across the restaurant to the hostess before Angie erupted.

She grabbed a passing busboy and hissed, "I'll give you a hundred bucks to dump ice water in his lap."

He glanced where she was pointing and then looked at her like she was nuts and said, "I can't get involved in marital disputes. You should probably take this up with your husband at home."

"He's not my husband," Mel protested but the busboy shook his head and scurried away.

"Have you lived in Scottsdale long?" Marty asked Elle.

"I —" Elle began, but whatever she'd been about to say was cut off as Angie popped out of her seat and yelled, "Stop it! Just stop it! You had your chance. I waited for you and waited for you, and did you ever notice me? No! Well, now somebody has noticed me, and I'm not going to walk away from him just because you think he isn't good enough for me."

Forks stopped in midair, glasses paused at lips, all eyes turned towards Tate and Angie. Mel lowered the wine list so she could see.

Angie was a vision. Her cheeks were flushed, her eyes sparked with fire. She was wearing a clingy Versace drape-front jersey dress in peacock blue. Her hair was twisted up into a knot, and she was wearing heels that added several inches to her height and made her legs look three miles long. She was stunning.

Tate's mouth sagged open. He blinked. He rose to his feet. He looked as if Angie had just punched him in the gut. Mel would have felt sorry for him if it wasn't his own stupid fault that he was in this mess.

"You waited for me?" he asked.

"Duh!" Angie snapped. "I've been in love with you since we were twelve years old."

"Sir . . . uh, Ma'am," the hostess interrupted, but everyone in the restaurant hushed her.

"You never said anything," Tate said.

"How could I when you've always been in love with someone else?"

Tate looked perplexed. "Who?"

"My best friend," Angie snapped.

"What?" Tate shook his head, rejecting her words.

"Oh, come on, she's your best friend, too, and she's standing right there!" Angie pointed at Mel.

Tate's head whipped in Mel's direction. His eyes bugged. Mel felt her eyes bug in return. A buzz began to fill the restaurant. Angie let out a sob and ran from the room.

"Angie!" Tate yelled after her. He glanced at Mel, and she gestured with her hand for him to go after her. He ran.

Mel glanced back at Marty. Elle was gazing at her with a shrewd glare.

She looked at Marty and said, "Wasn't that Tate Harper? The man who introduced us at the Biltmore? Odd that he's having dinner with Roach's girlfriend right next to us and her 'best friend' just happens to be lurking nearby. The same 'best friend' whose mother was dating my Baxter."

"Uh . . ." Marty stalled. He looked desperately at Mel and then said, "Help."

Mel approached their table, trying to weave together a basket of lies that would convince Elle that all of this was just a crazy coincidence. She wasn't that good of a basket weaver, however.

Elle rose to her feet and picked up her glass of champagne, which she tossed into Marty's face.

She sauntered past Mel and said, "Nice try, Melanie Cooper, but I'm on to you. Your mother is a suspect, but I'm not. I have an alibi. What does she have? Oh, yeah, nothing."

Mel could feel the entire restaurant watching her. She sidled over to Marty, who was dabbing champagne off of his dome with his napkin. With more dignity than she had in her little finger, he carefully rose, adjusted his lapels, and offered her his arm.

On their way out, Mel and Marty walked right into Detective Martinez. He was not happy to see them.

TWENTY-ONE

"Are you aware, Ms. Cooper, that we've had Elle Simpson under surveillance since the murder of Baxter Malloy?"

Mel was sitting in Detective Martinez's office while he paced back and forth and growled at her.

"Now, I don't care if you're dating the head of the FBI — stay away from my case. Do not follow anyone around, do not try to question anyone, in fact, do not leave your bakery — ever! Am I clear?"

"Crystal," Mel said.

"And that goes for you, too," Martinez snapped at Marty, who was sitting in the hard chair beside Mel.

Marty adjusted his cuffs and nodded.

A knock on the door interrupted them, and a silver head of hair appeared. Steve Wolfmeier. Mel stifled a groan.

"Detective Martinez," Steve said with his hand out. "I do believe I should be present if you're questioning my clients."

Martinez ignored Steve's hand and turned on Mel with one eyebrow raised. "You neglected to mention that you've retained legal services."

"No, I haven't," Mel said. "Mr. Wolfmeier is an acquaintance at best."

"Speak for yourself," Marty said. He looked at Steve. "Can you spring us?"

"Absolutely," Steve said, but Mel jumped up and interrupted.

"That's not necessary, is it, Detective?"

Martinez glared at her as if he'd like to lock her up for at least a week or two or until his case was solved.

"Is this where the party is being held?" Joe DeLaura pushed his way in around Steve.

Mel rushed across the room to give him a hug. "Thanks for coming."

"Detective, do you need Ms. Cooper or Mr. Zelaznik any longer?" Joe asked.

Mel wouldn't have thought it possible, but Martinez looked even more irritated than before.

"No, they're free to go, but I meant what I said, Ms. Cooper: Stay away from my case."

"Yes, sir," she said.

Joe ushered Marty and Mel out of the office.

"DeLaura, can I have a word?" Martinez asked.

Joe handed Mel his keys and said, "I'll meet you in the car."

"I'll walk you out, Melanie," Steve offered.

"That's not necessary," Joe said. He stepped between them and stood there until Mel and Marty began to walk away. Steve shrugged and leaned against the wall.

Mel took one last look over her shoulder, but Joe went into Martinez's office and shut the door behind him.

"What did you think you were going to accomplish by having Marty date one of the main suspects in Malloy's murder?" Joe asked.

"I was hoping Marty would find out something useful to pin on Elle," Mel said.

"Did you really think he was going to ply her with champagne, and she'd offer up a confession?"

"When you put it that way, it sounds ridiculous."

"That's because it *is* ridiculous!"

They were standing at the foot of the stairs that led up to Mel's apartment.

"You're not coming up, are you?" she asked.

"I can't," he said. He rubbed a hand over his face, and Mel saw how tired he looked. "I'm still sorting through some briefs for court tomorrow."

"I called you away to come help me," Mel said. "I'm sorry."

"It's all right," he said. He kissed the top of her head, and even though she knew he meant it in a comforting way, she couldn't help but feel even worse.

"Can I pack you some cupcakes?" she asked.

"No, but thanks," he said. "Look, I know you mean well, but you have to steer clear of this case. Martinez isn't kidding. If you get in his way again, even I won't be able to help you."

"Is that what he told you when he called you back to his office?"

Joe cocked his head to the side and studied her. "You are not fishing for information from me."

"Does that mean you don't have any?" she asked.

"Mel! You are the single most infuriating female I have ever met. You need to stay away from this case. Period."

"Tell that to my mother," Mel said. "She's

convinced the murderer is out to get her. She's a basket case, and she's driving me crazy."

"Uncle Stan can handle your mother," he said. "You need to focus on what you do best."

Mel blew out an exasperated breath. "Fine, I'll stay in the bakery."

"That would ease my mind tremendously," he said.

This time he kissed her on the lips and waited until she climbed the steps and let herself into her apartment.

As Mel brushed her teeth, she thought about their conversation. Technically speaking, staying in the kitchen didn't mean she wasn't going to keep asking questions. It just meant she'd have to do it from the bakery.

She prepped her bed and was just climbing in when there was a sharp knock on her door. She hurried across the room. Maybe Joe had finished working early and was going to stay over with her. She smoothed out her pajamas, wishing she'd picked her slinky nightie instead of her pink flannel set with cows, but it couldn't be helped.

She fluffed her hair and bit her lips as she hurried over to the door. She pulled aside the curtain, and her eyes widened in surprise. It wasn't Joe. It was Tate standing there.

She swiftly unlocked the deadbolt and ushered him in.

"What's going on? Did you catch up to Angie? Is everything okay?"

"I don't know, yes, and hell no," he said. He stomped past her and threw himself down on her bed.

"Okay, you don't know what's going on, you did catch up to Angie, but nothing is okay."

Tate put his hands over his eyes. He looked like he was in agony.

"I'm in love with her," he said.

Mel crossed the room and plopped down beside him.

"No duh."

"You know? How?" He lowered his arms to look at her.

"Would you really be trying to break up her and Roach if you weren't?"

"No," he said. "She thinks I'm in love with you."

"I know," Mel sighed.

"I'm not," he said. He looked at her as if he was worried she'd be offended. Mel laughed.

"I know that, too," she said. "I tried to tell her, but she doesn't believe me."

"Me, either," he said.

"What are you going to do?" Mel asked.

"What can I do?" he asked. "She's dating someone else."

"You could tell her how you feel," Mel said.

"What if she rejects me?"

"What if she doesn't?"

Tate was silent, staring up at the ceiling.

"What have you got to lose?" Mel asked.

"Her," he said.

Tate left a short while later. Mel wished she could make everything turn out all right for her friends, but she didn't know what that meant. Tate and Angie together? With other people? *Sheesh!* She was barely keeping her own relationship out of the morgue.

Instead, she turned her mind to Baxter Malloy's murder. Someone had strangled the man with her mother's stocking. That was an act of rage if ever there was one. Of course, given Malloy's shady business dealings, there were more suspects than she knew what to do with, and she suspected Detective Martinez felt the same way, which was probably why he was so cranky all of the time.

If the Hargraves had done it, it seemed odd that they would stay in town to bunk with family, especially family that was enjoying their downfall with such glee.

There was a long list of stiffed investors to comb through, but again, murder seemed harsh when litigation might have gotten them some if not all of their money back. Which brought Mel back to Roach.

He and his father were estranged. They hadn't spoken in years, and yet Roach just happened to be in town when his father was murdered. And not just murdered but *strangled.* It would take physical strength to accomplish that, which Roach as a drummer certainly had. Then again, Angie was sure of his alibi. Mel hoped fervently that she was right. She didn't want Angie to be hurt or, even worse, in danger.

So, who else had a passionate reason to kill Baxter Malloy? Elle Simpson, Malloy's bodacious girlfriend.

She had been following Mel and her mother the day they went shopping for a dress, which meant she knew about the date. She had been checking out the competition, no doubt. Could she have gotten so angry about being removed from Malloy's bankroll that she killed him?

Mel had seen her temper at the museum luncheon for herself. Elle was a tad high-strung. She was certainly young enough and fit enough to have taken on Malloy, especially if she surprised him.

If only Angie and Tate hadn't had their blowout in the restaurant. Marty might have been able to get something useful out of Elle. *Damn.*

A small, private service was held at Messinger Mortuary and Chapel. A minister gave a short sermon, and Roach offered a brief eulogy. There was only a handful of people in attendance: Angie, Mel, the band, and their crew. None of Baxter's contemporaries made an appearance, which was not surprising, given that he had ripped off everyone he had ever known.

Sadly, it wasn't a celebration of a life lived well, but rather a lesson in how not to go. Mel wondered if Baxter had ever imagined his own passing, and if so, if he had pictured it like this.

When the service was over, Roach stood by his father's casket and received hugs and handshakes. He looked ill at ease, and Mel had to wonder if it was guilt that made him squirm so.

Detective Martinez had crept in halfway through the service, and Mel had noticed that Roach's leg began to bounce up and down, as if he had become agitated at the sight of the detective. Was he nervous? Was

Martinez here to arrest him?

Mel glanced at Angie, but she had eyes only for her man. If she was worried about the detective's presence, it didn't show.

"Stop!" a screech came from the doorway. "I demand that you stop!"

Mel turned towards the door. Ringed by paparazzi with flashbulbs popping was Elle Simpson.

TWENTY-TWO

"I was the love of Baxter's life!" Elle declared. "How dare you shut me out of his funeral?"

The entire room stood slack-jawed and staring. One of the funeral directors raced forward to slam the door on the photographers, but not before a full-on flashbulb assault left them all seeing spots.

Roach recovered first. He was still standing by the casket, but now he turned and faced Elle.

"No, you weren't. My mother was the love of his life, and you could never replace her."

Elle clapped her hands over her prominent bosom as if she'd been shot. "Who has been his constant companion for the past three years? Me. Not you, his estranged son."

Mel glanced past Elle to see Detective Martinez watching the encounter like it was a tennis match.

"My relationship with my father is none

of your damn business."

"I loved him. That makes it my business. And you have to admit it's awfully convenient that you're here in town, completely broke, your father's sole heir, and — oh! — he gets murdered." Elle made a face of mock alarm.

"What exactly are you trying to say, Elle?" Roach looked at her as if he'd happily strangle her, and Mel realized that was a disturbing choice of imagery.

"Oh, nothing much." She shrugged. "Just pointing out that you feel a lot of rage towards your father. How is it you two became estranged?"

"I really can't remember," Roach said. "Over something small and petty, no doubt."

"No doubt," Elle agreed. Then her lips turned up in what might have been a smile if it weren't so calculating and cold. "Oh, wait — I was dating *you,* and you caught Baxter and me in bed together. Terrible scene that night, if I recall."

"Funny," he said, his voice as dry as dust. "I don't remember a thing."

He was cool, but the damage was done. Angie was frowning, and Detective Martinez looked like he'd just won the lottery.

Mel studied Elle. Why was she bringing

this up now? If she was so convinced that Roach had killed his father, she could have mentioned this before. Mel didn't believe that she was hurt to have been left out of the funeral arrangements. She doubted that Elle cared about that at all. In fact, the only thing she thought Elle might care about was being left out of the will.

"I think you should go," Angie said. She stepped in front of Roach as if to protect him from Elle.

Elle foolishly made the mistake of dismissing Angie as a person of no importance.

"Who asked you?" Elle snapped.

"No one had to," Angie said.

She was wearing a black sheath dress with white piping along the collar and hem. Her brown hair was up in an Audrey Hepburn twist, and her skinny-heeled black pumps gave her at least four more inches of height than normal. She was the very image of a lady, until Mel noticed she was clenching her right fist.

Mel stepped up beside Angie and looped her arm through hers. "Thank you for paying your respects, Ms. Simpson. We need to be moving along to the cemetery now. Right?"

Roach stood glaring at Elle. She glared back. Mel wondered how long this was going to go on. Finally, she pinched Angie to get her moving.

"Ouch!" Angie gave her an irritated look.

Mel shooed her in the direction of Roach. Angie took the hint and put her hand on his arm. "Are you ready, sweetheart?"

Mel had a feeling the endearment was for Elle's sake, and she marveled again at Angie's fierce loyalty to those she cared about. It had to shock her to know that Elle was Roach's former girlfriend.

She looked at them, and he lowered his head to Angie's and whispered something in her ear. She smiled at him. Then again, maybe he had already told her. Mel could only imagine what Tate was going to have to say about this turn of events.

Roach straightened his spine and glanced at Elle. "Thanks for your condolences."

He kissed Angie's hand and went to his spot at the casket. The band surrounded the casket with him, and together they carried it to the hearse outside.

Elle was forced to move aside or be bowled over by the polished wooden box. Photographers waited outside, but the band was oblivious as they loaded the casket and climbed into a waiting limo.

Mel and Angie walked out together. Roach was waiting by the limo for Angie, and Mel gave her a quick squeeze before she hurried over to join him. Mel watched the door shut behind them. One of the photographers got too close, and the limo driver was forced to push him back so he could shut the door.

"I hope she's not measuring the curtains," Elle jeered as she moved to stand beside Mel.

Mel turned to look at her. Mel wasn't generally a violent person, but there was something about Elle that made her fingers itch to slap the woman.

"I'm sure I don't know what you mean."

"The Malloy men are fickle," Elle said. "Whatever this is between them, it won't last."

"I'd like a word with you, Ms. Simpson," Detective Martinez said.

Mel had never thought she'd be so glad to see him.

"I don't have time right now," Elle protested.

"Make the time," he said.

"So then what happened?" Tate demanded.

"I don't know," Mel said. "I came here to open the bakery."

They were standing in the main room of the bakery while Mel restocked the cases.

"When is Angie going to get here?" he asked.

"I don't know," she said. "They were doing a private graveside service and then going back to Baxter's house. I just assumed she'd be taking the day off."

Marty bustled in from the back room, carrying another tray of Cherry Bomb Cupcakes. The Valentine's Day crush had begun, and Mel wasn't even bothering to bake anything that wasn't red, white, or pink, unless it was a special order.

"When are you going to do the drawing?" he asked.

He was wearing the Armani suit beneath his apron, and Mel wondered if he was ever going to take it off. She had a feeling he had become overly attached to his new threads.

"Tomorrow," she said. "Right after our final couples' cooking class."

He pumped his fist, and Mel shook her head.

"You know, a lot of people have entered," she said. "You may not win."

He grinned at her. "I have a gut feeling about this. So good, in fact, that I've already asked Beatriz and she said yes."

"Oh, Marty." Mel bit her lip.

"Don't worry," he said. "My gut is never wrong."

He hurried back to the kitchen and Mel gave Tate a worried look.

"You're going to have to put him on the payroll," Tate said. "Especially, if he's planning to borrow more of my suits."

"Oh, you recognized it, did you?"

"It wasn't hard," Tate said. "I'm happy to contribute to the cause, but next time let me pick the giveaway."

"Absolutely," Mel said. "Sorry about that."

"So, do you think Angie is going to dump Roach over the Elle situation?" he asked. He sounded hopeful.

"I don't know. It was a surprise, but it was also years ago."

"Why do you suppose the police haven't arrested either Elle or Roach?" Tate asked. "Obviously, they have the strongest motives."

"They must have really good alibis," Mel said.

Tate was still for a moment. "You don't think . . . ?"

"What?" Mel asked. She glanced up from where she was arranging cupcakes in the display case when he didn't answer right away. "Tate, what are you thinking?"

He stared at her, but Mel got the feeling he wasn't really seeing her.

"Nothing," he said. "Listen, I've got to go. Do me a favor?"

"Sure."

"Call me when Ange gets in," he said. "I'm worried about her."

"Will do," Mel said. She watched as he disappeared through the door. She had a feeling he wasn't telling her everything.

The bells on the door chimed, and Mel glanced up, hoping to see Angie. Instead, a woman in an overly large sun hat, enormous celebrity-style sunglasses, and a gray trench coat entered the bakery. She had long dark hair that was at odds with her gently lined face. It looked like a bad dye job or a wig.

Mel was silent for a moment. Then she heaved a sigh.

"Mom, what are you doing?" she asked.

"Shh," Joyce hushed her. "I'm incognito."

"Not really. I mean, if I recognized you, that should tell you something," Mel said.

"You're my daughter," Joyce said as she lowered her glasses to peer over the tops. "Of course you recognized me."

"Is there something happening, Mom, that you need a disguise?"

"The murderer is after me," Joyce said. "I'm sure of it. I feel eyes upon me wherever

I go, and I saw strange footprints in the backyard."

"Those could be Charlie's," Mel said, trying to calm her mother down. She had so been hoping that her mother wouldn't find those footprints.

"He doesn't wear shoes like that," Joyce said. "Now listen, I don't want you to worry . . ."

The front door chimed, and Mel glanced up. Looking as suave as ever, Jay Gatwick strolled in and smiled at her.

"Afternoon, Melanie," he said. "You're looking as lovely as a freshly picked rose."

Mel laughed. "Flattery will get you free cupcakes."

"Just speaking the truth," he said. "I believe you have an order for Poppy's book club."

"It's in back," Mel said. "I'll just go grab it."

When she returned, Jay was trying to make small talk with her mother, who had pulled down the brim of her hat and was ignoring him.

"Jay, this is my . . ."

"Myra," her mother interrupted. She kept her face averted and held out her hand to Jay. "Myra Streusel."

Mel wondered if it was obvious to Jay that

her mother had just read her made-up last name off of the menu board. Probably.

"A pleasure," Jay said. He returned her handshake.

"If you'll excuse us a moment," Joyce said. She tugged Mel over to the side and whispered, "Listen, I have to go. I'm going underground until all of this blows over."

"Underground?" Mel asked. "Where? In that old bomb shelter in your yard?"

"No, that's just an expression," Joyce said. "You can reach me at my cell number. Ginny and I are going to a spa under assumed names."

"And you'd tell me where, but then you'd have to kill me," Mel said.

"Laugh if you must," Joyce said. Her tone made it clear she was feeling injured by Mel's lack of dramatic concern.

"I'm not laughing, Mo — *Myra,*" Mel said. She hugged her mom tight. "Go with Ginny and be safe. I'll call you if I hear anything on this end. Does Uncle Stan know your plan?"

"Yes," Joyce said. She hugged Mel back hard. "I'll be in touch. Remember, no matter what happens, I love you."

"I love you, too," Mel said. She watched her mother go and shook her head. She wished she was going to hide out at a spa for a few days. Then she wouldn't have to deal with Angie and Tate and Marty and the contest . . . oh, yeah, and the murderer who seemed intent on messing up the lives of everyone Mel cared about.

"Is everything okay?" Jay asked.

Mel glanced up. "Yes, sorry. I'm a little preoccupied."

"I don't mean to pry, but wasn't that your mother?"

A laugh burst out of Mel before she could stop it.

"Sorry," she said. "It's just that Mom is trying to be in disguise. She'd be dreadfully disappointed that someone who met her only once was able to identify her."

"Oh, well, I could only do it because she was standing next to you. You're the spitting image of her." Then he raised one eyebrow and said, "Forgive me for asking, but why does she need a disguise?"

"She's convinced that Malloy's murderer is after her," Mel said.

"Has something happened?" he asked. "She should have protection."

"My Uncle Stan is keeping a close eye on her," Mel said.

"Still, a murderer on the loose is disturbing. Poor Poppy is still having night terrors about it."

"Oh, I'm sorry," Mel said. "Give her my best, won't you?"

"Absolutely."

"No!" Angie slammed through the front door. The bells clanged as if disturbed from a nap. Both Mel and Jay started at the noise.

"Angie, I can explain," Roach said. "Detective Martinez got to Elle. That's why she crashed the funeral. She's scared, and she's trying to make me look guilty."

He was following behind her, but she spun around and held up her hand.

"No, I don't want to hear it! There's a big difference between 'I was comforting a friend the night my father was murdered' and 'I was with a former girlfriend the night my father was murdered.' "

Mel's eyes went wide. Roach had been with a former girlfriend on the night his father was killed? Elle?

"Well, I'm just going to . . ." Jay trailed off as he scooped up his cupcakes and headed towards the door.

Mel couldn't blame him. Angie looked so angry, Mel half expected volcanic ash to begin raining down upon them.

"You lied to me!" Angie said.

"No, I didn't!" Roach argued. "Look, Elle showed up at my hotel saying she and my father had broken up. She was distraught. I

292

tried to console her. That's all."

Angie glared at him. "Define *console.*"

"What?" he asked.

"Was the consoling done with clothes on or off?"

"On!" Roach put a hand over his heart. "I swear on my life, on your life, on Mel's life . . ."

"Hey, leave me out of this," Mel said.

"If you're lying, Roach Malloy, I will put an evil eye on you for the rest of your days that will shrivel your privates and turn your drumming muscles into rhythmless noodles," Angie warned.

He looked duly impressed. "I'm not lying. Look, I know we just met, and it's been under unusual circumstances, but I am crazy about you. I will never do anything to jeopardize what we've got. I promise."

Angie looked somewhat mollified. Roach pulled her into his arms and kissed her. Mel looked away just as Marty came back through the kitchen door.

"Oh, she decided to show up," he said. "Good. I have a yoga class to get to." He took off his apron and tossed it on the counter. "See you tomorrow."

"Bye, Marty."

Angie and Roach disconnected at the lip, and he smoothed back her hair and said,

"Will you still think about what I asked you?"

"Yes, but it's so sudden," she said.

"I'm just asking you to think about it," he said. "For me, please?"

She nodded. He gave her another swift kiss before he left with a wave.

"Well, looks like the graveside service was informative."

"I need a cupcake," Angie said. She went into the kitchen and Mel followed.

"So, Roach and Elle are each other's alibis," Mel said.

Angie went into the cooler and came back out with two Kiss Me Cupcakes. She sat at the steel worktable and unwrapped them. She finished off the first one before she acknowledged Mel's question.

"Yes, Elle and Roach were together at his hotel the night that Baxter was murdered. Given their past, you can imagine how much the police love that. Fortunately, they spent most of the night in the lobby bar and have plenty of witnesses. However, Roach thinks Detective Martinez got to Elle, because now she's saying that there is a twenty-minute time gap where she can't vouch for his whereabouts."

"That's not good."

"To put it mildly," Angie said, taking a

bite out of cupcake number two.

"But you believe they didn't sleep together?" Mel took the seat beside her.

Angie thought about it for a second and then said, "Yes."

"But how can you be so sure?" Mel asked.

"I can't," she said. "But whatever happened was before I met him, so I don't really know that it's my business. Besides, everything has changed now."

"Why?"

"Because Roach has asked me to move back to Los Angeles with him."

TWENTY-THREE

"And you said . . . ?"

"That I needed to think about it," Angie answered. "It's a big decision."

"I'll say," Mel said. "What about the business?"

"I was thinking we could open another shop in LA," Angie said. "Or you could come with me."

"But our family and friends are all here," Mel said. "And the bakery is just beginning to take off."

"I know," Angie said. She sounded agonized. "But for the first time in my life, I feel adored just for being me. I don't want to give that up, either."

A million reasons why she shouldn't go leapt to Mel's tongue, but she kept her mouth shut. Angie was her best friend. It would be like severing an arm to let her go, but if Angie had found real happiness with Roach, then Mel had no right to ask her not to go.

"Whatever you decide is okay with me," she said.

Angie looked as if she might cry, so Mel hugged her tight. The string of bells on the door jangled, so Mel pulled back and said, "Sit and relax. I'll go man the front."

Angie nodded and Mel left her to her thoughts. She didn't even want to think about how Tate was going to take this news.

After Angie dumped flour instead of sugar into the buttercream frosting and then put blue food coloring into what was supposed to be red velvet batter, Mel sent her home. It was obvious Angie had more on her mind than baking, and Mel figured she'd better go before she blew something up.

In the silence of the bakery, while she wiped down the tables and restocked the napkin holders, she thought about what the place would be like without Angie. It wasn't a pleasant thought. She'd have to hire Marty full time, and as much as she'd grown to like him, it wouldn't be the same.

And even though Roach said Elle had turned against him because Detective Martinez was pressuring her, he was still the best possible candidate for his father's murder. How was Mel ever going to sleep again if her best friend moved to LA with a man who could very well be a murderer?

She could only hope that Roach was as innocent as Angie believed him to be. And it was possible. Baxter had made a lot of enemies. Still, the fact that there was twenty minutes of time for which Elle couldn't verify Roach's whereabouts . . . *Wait.* If she couldn't verify his whereabouts, did that mean no one could verify hers?

Baxter was strangled. If it was a crime of passion, Elle was the most likely suspect unless, like Jay had speculated before, there was more than one person involved. A cold knot of dread formed in Mel's stomach. She felt like smacking her forehead. Of course! How perfect: Roach and Elle had done it together. They both said they were in the bar at his hotel, and plenty of witnesses could place them there.

But he'd been staying at The Phoenician, only minutes from his father's house. He could easily have left, strangled his father, and made it back in time to cement his alibi. Or maybe it was Elle. She could have left, killed Baxter, and made it back herself. Perhaps they had planned it together, but Roach's sudden relationship with Angie had gummed up the works. Maybe Elle had planned to share more than murder with Roach, and now she was angry enough about his new relationship to let him take all of the blame.

But how had they known that Baxter would be at his house? Elle knew he'd had a date planned. But Mel's mother had told her that stopping back at Baxter's had been a spontaneous idea. They were supposed to be at a show at the Civic Center, but had ditched their plans to go hot tubbing.

So, it couldn't be Elle or Roach, unless they had been following Joyce and Baxter, which they couldn't have been if they were in the hotel bar all evening.

Mel slammed down a napkin holder. This was maddening. Someone had murdered Baxter Malloy, and it had to be someone who knew he'd had a date with her mother.

So who knew her mother had a date with Baxter? Angie, herself, her mother's friend Ginny, Joe, and Tate. And her favorite suspect, Elle, but that was a wash now that she had an alibi. Mel thought back to the night her mother had told her about her date with Malloy. If she could do it all over again, she'd tell her not to go.

But then she remembered how excited Joyce had been, showing up to her class in her pajamas to announce she had a date. Mel felt the cold knot in the pit of her stomach again. Her students had heard about Joyce's date. Could it be someone from her class? She didn't like to think it, but how could she not?

Her cell phone rang in the silence. She glanced at the number. It was Tate. Uh-oh.

"Hello," she said.

"Los Angeles," he said. "She's actually considering it."

"I know."

"What should I do?"

"I don't know," Mel said. "I don't even know what to do myself."

"I'm going to tell her how I feel," he said.

Mel was silent. Angie had been in love with Tate for more than twenty years. Would this get her to stay? Or would this make things awkward and bust apart their friendship for good?

"You're not saying anything," Tate said. "You think I shouldn't tell her."

"I don't know what to think," Mel said. "Why couldn't you have figured out how you felt about her two weeks ago? Then we wouldn't be in this mess."

"So, it's my fault she took up with a rock star," he said.

"Yes, it is," Mel said. "Why do men have to be so stupid? Why can't they just get it done?"

"Don't yell at me because Joe is dropping

the ball in the romance department," Tate said.

"This is not about me and Joe," Mel snapped.

"Have you slept together yet?"

"That's none of your business."

"I thought not," he snapped in return.

"Tate, don't take this the wrong way, but I'm hanging up on you."

"Wait! What should I do about Angie?"

"Remember what you said about *Casablanca*? He never should have let her get on that plane. Now man up!" Mel said.

She clicked her phone shut. This was the downside to cell phones. It was nowhere near as satisfying to press end as it was to slam a phone into its holder.

She locked up the bakery and trudged up to bed. Joe had called earlier and said he was working late. Tomorrow was her last couples' cupcake class. If someone in her class had overheard her mother's date plans, this would be her only opportunity to see who in class may have had a motive to murder Baxter Malloy, and she wasn't going to blow it.

"Why are you so jittery?" Angie asked.

"Too much coffee," Mel lied.

Angie had arrived to work with dark

circles under her eyes, and Mel was guessing she hadn't slept much. She didn't say whether she had talked to Tate or not, so Mel was guessing Tate hadn't told her how he felt. She didn't want to add to Angie's personal crisis, so she said nothing about the fact that she suspected someone in their class might have whacked Malloy.

The truth was that the class was to start in fifteen minutes, and Mel was nervous. She had spent the morning making calls, and discovered more than she wanted to about her students.

Mr. Felix had mentioned before that his company had invested his pension with Malloy's company, and sure enough, when Mel checked, the company had lost the entire pension fund. When she had asked Mr. Felix about it, he had been so angry. They were an elderly couple, so Mel didn't really see them strangling Malloy, but maybe they knew someone younger and stronger. It was a scary thought.

The Bickersons — rather, the Bakersons — were connected, too, and not just because the Hargraves, their cousins, had lost everything by investing it with Malloy. Dan had been employed by the accounting company Malloy's investment firm had used. He worked for them for less than a year, having been let go just before he passed probation.

Mel wondered what could have happened to result in his termination. She also wondered if the Hargraves had been directed by him to invest with Malloy. If Dan had known that Malloy was operating a Ponzi scheme, seeing the cousins lose the inheritance they'd swindled from his wife would be the ultimate revenge.

The Dunns and the Koslowskis didn't have a connection, being from out of town. But the Gatwicks moved in the same social circle as Malloy. Mel didn't really see any other tie to Malloy, but still, they had been there the night her mother had announced her date. As far as Mel was concerned, everyone was a suspect.

She placed tonight's cupcakes on a cupcake tower in the middle of the steel worktable. They were making heart-shaped cupcakes called Love Me Knots, chocolate cake with amaretto buttercream frosting. Right now, she wished she could eat about five of them, but she restrained herself. Barely.

She and Angie hadn't spoken much today. There was an awkwardness between them that Mel had never felt before. She knew it was because she was trying very hard not to influence Angie's decision, and the only way to keep herself from saying "please don't go" was to keep her mouth shut.

The Bickersons were the first in the door, per usual. Mel braced herself for a round of squabbling from the couple, but she found herself doing a double take. Dan was holding Irene's hand, and they were beaming at each other. Apparently, torturing the Hargraves was better than therapy for them.

Angie gave Mel a wide-eyed look over the couples' heads, and Mel returned it.

"Hi, Irene, Dan," she said. "How are you two tonight?"

"Wonderful, just wonderful," Irene gushed and gave Dan a smacking kiss on the cheek. He turned bright red but looked pleased all the same.

"Here you go, my dear," he said and pulled a chair out for her.

"Oh, thank you, hon."

While they put on their aprons, the Koslowskis and the Dunns arrived. While greetings were exchanged, Angie sidled up to Mel and said, "Can you believe that?"

"No."

"How long do you think revenge can keep them together?"

"When it comes with free domestic labor and yard work, I'm betting for a while."

"I've dated men for less," Angie agreed.

"Hey, did you have a chance to go over the payments for the classes? Since it's the last class, we should probably make sure that declined payment went through."

"Oh, nuts. It's been so crazy, I completely forgot. I'll go look at it now. Can you start class without me?"

"Sure. Neither the Felixes nor the Gatwicks are here yet. Should I start without them?"

"Yes, we can help them catch up when they get here."

Mel crossed the kitchen and ducked into her office. It was little more than a closet, but she didn't need much more than basic office equipment.

She picked up the manila folder that held all of the registration and payment information for her couples' class. She sifted through the papers until she found the one with a bright pink Post-it on it. Angie had noted the date and time that she had run the transaction. It had been declined.

Mel looked at the information. It was for the Gatwicks. That couldn't be right. The Gatwicks were loaded; everyone knew that. She felt herself go still. *Unless they weren't.*

She remembered the charity luncheon, the women talking about how wonderful Jay Gatwick was and how he spoiled Poppy. But what if they were wrong? What if Jay Gatwick was broke? And what if he was broke because he had invested with Baxter Malloy? Would that drive him to murder?

She remembered his face when her mother had announced her date with Malloy. She had thought he was offended by Joyce's appearance in her pajamas, but what if that wasn't it? What if he'd been interested, *too* interested?

She needed to call Uncle Stan. He would be able to contact Detective Martinez and find out if the Gatwicks had lost money to Malloy. She hadn't seen any connection between Gatwick and Malloy other than a social one, but maybe she'd missed something. She decided not to call from the office, as she might be overheard. She picked up her cell phone and stepped out into the bakery.

She caught Angie's eye and gestured that she needed to make a call. Angie nodded. Mel slipped out the back door. This shouldn't take long, and then she could duck back into class.

She stepped out into the alley and opened her contacts list. Uncle Stan was alphabetically at the bottom, and she scrolled down until his name popped up. She was about to press the call button when a hand reached around her and snatched her phone. "I wouldn't do that if I were you."

Twenty-Four

Mel gasped and spun around. Jay Gatwick was standing there looking as squeaky-suave as Ryan Seacrest in a dark suit and highly buffed shoes. Mel noted they were narrow at the toe and had a small heel. The hair on the back of her neck prickled in alarm.

"You startled me," she said. "What are you doing back here?"

"I've been watching you," he said. "I knew it was only a matter of time before you figured it out."

"I'm not sure what you mean," Mel bluffed. "Here, we really should be getting into class. The others will wonder what's become of us."

"You maybe, not me," Jay said. "Poppy called earlier and left a message on your voice mail to say we wouldn't be able to make it tonight. She's feeling under the weather. In fact, I left her sleeping and, given the sedative she took, I'm sure she'll believe I was home with her the entire time."

"What do you want?" Mel asked.

"For the moment, I need to make sure you don't make any calls to that uncle of yours," he said. "Come, let's go upstairs where we can talk. And don't try to signal anyone in the kitchen. I'd hate to have to harm so many innocent people."

Mel knew she shouldn't go, but the lethal-looking gun Jay pulled out of his pocket made her reconsider. Well, that and she hated the thought of putting the rest of her students and Angie in harm's way. She'd just have to try to bluff her way out.

"Shall we?" he said. He gestured up the stairs towards her apartment.

"Angie will be expecting me to return," she said.

"Too bad you're going to call her first and tell her you have to run a quick errand. Meanwhile, you'll sadly expire from a carbon monoxide leak in your little apartment."

"Do you really think people are going to believe that?" Mel asked.

"Well, you did seem awfully depressed that your relationship with the assistant district attorney was moving so slowly. Have you two even slept together yet?"

Mel gritted her teeth. "None of your business."

"I thought not," he said. "Poppy has a friend — what's her name? — oh yeah, Susan Ross. Beautiful woman. She works with your boyfriend and apparently everyone in his office knows that you two aren't all that. I'm sure Susan will be happy to comfort him through his time of grief."

Mel felt her temper surge. If she ever got out of this, she was going to jump on Joe and not let the man up until they were officially shacked up.

She reached the door to her apartment and fumbled for her key. Her fingers were cold and clumsy. Jay sighed impatiently, and she feared he might shoot her just to be done with it. She turned the lock and pushed the door open.

As she stepped into her apartment, she became immediately aware of two things. First, someone was in her apartment already, and second, the gun at her back lowered, probably in surprise.

Rose petals covered the floor, her futon had been made up with gold satin sheets, champagne and chocolates sat on the counter, candles were burning all over the room, and jazz was playing on the stereo. It was beautiful, romantic, lovely, and perfect.

The bathroom door opened and out stepped Joe, drying his hair with a towel while another was draped loosely around his hips.

He paused, as if suddenly sensing he wasn't alone. He lowered the towel and glanced at Mel and Jay and said, "You're here. And you're not alone. That was not really a part of my plan."

"Mine either," Jay said dryly.

Mel knew Jay would kill them both. He had too much to lose. She had to act fast. She ducked away from Jay and dashed around the futon to stand in front of Joe.

"You can't kill us both," she said.

"Are you kidding?" Jay asked and then laughed. It wasn't a pleasant sound. "This is like a gift from above. Look at this place. It looks like one of those cheap hour-rate motels on Van Buren Street in Phoenix."

"Hey!" Joe protested.

"Think of it," Jay continued. "The lovers finally get together, and *kaboom!* How terrifically tragic."

"He's going to blow us up?" Joe asked Mel. "Why?"

"He killed Baxter Malloy," she said. "And I figured it out."

"Naturally, it wouldn't be a date with you without some sort of life-threatening drama," Joe said.

"Is that a slam?" Mel asked. "Because, really, I don't think this is my fault."

"Of course it's your fault," Jay cut in. He waved the gun at them, motioning for them to sit on the couch. "You couldn't leave it alone, could you? Oh, no, you had to crash the charity luncheon, you had to chase down the Hargraves, you had to keep asking questions, your partner had to start dating the perfect fall guy. You ruined everything."

"How is killing us going to help you?" Mel asked. She laced her fingers through Joe's. Feeling his warmth gave her strength. "You're still broke."

"Ah, yes, but with you gone, I'll be able to pin the murder on someone else. And then I'll go back to doing what I was so good at before it all fell apart."

"What's that?" Joe asked.

"Blackmail," Jay said. "I'm not so stupid as to invest in Baxter's Ponzi scheme, but once I caught on to what he was up to, I realized I had a much more reliable way of making money. Baxter had to pay up, or I'd out him to his clients and the SEC. I must say, it was quite lucrative while it lasted."

"Then why did you kill him?" Mel asked.

"That was an accident," Jay said. "I was

trying to convince him to resume his payments. He said he didn't have the money, but was hoping to hook up with a rich widow soon. The fool thought your mother was loaded. In my ire at his stupidity, I got carried away. It was an unfortunate miscalculation."

"You strangled a man to death," Mel snapped. "That's not a miscalculation."

Joe squeezed her fingers as if trying to calm her. But Mel didn't feel calm. She felt like grabbing the nearest heavy object and smacking Jay Gatwick upside the head with it.

"You have been following my mother, haven't you?"

"I had to be sure she didn't see me that night," he said.

"What if she had?" Mel asked.

He shrugged. Mel took that to mean it would be Joyce who'd be gassed or blown to bits. She felt her body begin to tremble, but she wasn't sure if it was fear or rage.

She had thought Jay was her friend, trying to help her figure out who had killed Malloy, when all along he'd been stalking her mother and using her for information.

"What's the fuss? It wasn't as if Malloy was a great guy," Jay said. "He was a con man. Do you think any of his investors are sad that he's gone? Frankly, they should all pay me a pest-removal fee."

"So, your plan now is to kill us?" Joe said. "I can tell you as a DA that you could plead Malloy's murder, but you won't be able to do that if you murder us."

"That's okay," Jay said. "I'm not planning on getting caught. You know the story about how Poppy and I met in Italy, and I decided I had to marry her. Well, that's only half of the story.

"You see, I let people believe I was the son of wealthy Swiss parents, who had sadly been killed in a plane crash. In reality, I was working my way around Europe as a pick-pocket. It can be a cushy income if you're quick with your fingers and know how to blend into the crowd.

"Then one day, I saw Poppy walking along the street without a care in the world. Only people with money can walk like that, and I knew that was what I wanted. I wanted her, and I wanted that life. So, I charmed her and her parents, and as I got to know the members of their world, I realized that so many of them had so much to hide. Infidelity, addictions, dark family secrets — they were all ripe for the picking, and I was the king of the orchard.

"That's how I began gathering my wealth,

and I needed to be wealthy. You see, Poppy is like a flawless diamond. She comes at a price, and if a man can't pay the price, he can't have Poppy.

"But then, I met Baxter Malloy. He tried to talk me into investing with him, but I knew he was a con man like me. So, I studied him, and I watched him, and then when I knew I had enough proof to black-mail him, well, then the big money started rolling in. It was beautiful."

"Until you killed him," Mel said.

"Hmm, pity," Jay agreed.

"Well, as fascinating as all of this is, could a guy at least put on some pants before he dies?" Joe asked.

This time Mel squeezed Joe's hand to keep him calm.

Jay tipped his head and considered them. "No, I think it's better this way. In fact, Melanie, you need to lose some clothes. Hey, at least everyone will think you two are finally getting it on."

Joe looked at Mel and shook his head. "Does everyone know?"

Mel shrugged.

Joe gave her a small smile. "That was the plan for tonight, by the way."

"Everything looks lovely," she said. "Thank you."

Joe looked into her eyes, and Mel was struck by how much she loved him. It caught her by surprise, and she gasped. She had always had a crush on him, she had always lusted after him, but somewhere in the past few months she'd fallen in love with him, head over heels, from the bottom of her heart in love.

Joe gave her a slow smile. "I feel the same way," he said.

"All right, break it up," Jay snapped. "I'm on a schedule here."

Joe gave Mel's hand one last squeeze before he let go.

"You don't really think I'm going to let you harm her, do you?" Joe grabbed his towel in one hand and stood. He turned to face Jay.

"How do you propose to stop me?"

Mel had never been athletic. During her first and only beach volleyball game, she'd gotten spiked on the head with a ball and was rendered unconscious. Softball had been a dual humiliation entailing striking out repeatedly and getting hit in the booty with a slow pitch, which slow or not still hurt like the devil and left her with a purple butt cheek.

However, this was more life and death than volleyball or softball. There was a candle within reach, and it was burning in a chunky glass votive she'd picked up at the Denmarket furniture store. If she could grab it and by some miracle hit Jay with it, she and Joe might stand a chance.

The next few seconds happened in an adrenaline-fueled blur that Mel would never be able to fully recall, as she retained only strobe-flash memories of the events.

She grabbed the candle in her right hand. Joe made a sudden leap across the back of the futon at Jay. Jay jumped back in shock. Mel threw the candle as hard as she could, but now Joe was in the line of fire, and the heavy glass struck him on the shoulder. He landed with a *splat* on the floor. Jay was so busy watching him that he didn't see the candle continue its trajectory until it hit him in the throat. He dropped his gun and landed on his knees, grabbing his throat and making harsh, guttural animal noises.

Joe shot forward and snatched up the gun. Mel thought she had never seen anything as splendid as Joe buck naked and clutching a gun. The smell of smoke brought her back to her senses, and she shrieked when she saw the lick of flame from the candle igniting her fluffy area rug.

Joe let loose a string of curses and reached over the couch to grab his towel, which he used to beat at the flames. Mel raced to the kitchen and grabbed her water pitcher out of the fridge. She yanked off the top and poured it on the flames. They were extinguished with a hiss.

The back door flew open, and there stood Angie. She took in the scene with wide eyes.

"Joe!" she cried. "Naked in Mel's apartment. Well, it's about time."

Several hours passed before Detective Martinez was finished asking questions. He seemed particularly interested in the fact that Joe was naked when the incident occurred. While Joe seemed to find this an affirmation of his manliness and confirmation of their relationship, Mel found it mortifying.

Uncle Stan, Tate, and Angie all loitered around Mel's apartment. They watched as Jay was hauled away, and they all agreed not to call Joyce and ruin her spa time until the next day.

In the aftermath of her adrenaline burst, Mel felt suddenly tired and could no longer hold back the yawns that were overtaking her. As if sensing that she was at her end, Joe ushered everyone out of the apartment.

"Champagne?" he asked as he closed and locked the door behind them.

"That sounds lovely," Mel said. She eased back onto the futon and rested her head. She and Joe were finally alone, the murderer had been caught, and all was right with the world once more. She yawned again.

She watched through eyes heavy-lidded with exhaustion as Joe hefted the bottle out of the melted ice and untwisted the wire holder. He covered the cork with his left palm and pushed with his right thumb. A satisfying *pop* sounded, and he stopped the cork from doing any damage.

He poured the bubbly beverage into the two waiting glass flutes and put the bottle back in the ice bucket. As she watched him, Mel saw him moving his mouth as if talking to himself. She wondered if he was giving himself a pep talk, or maybe he was just practicing for the courtroom.

She stretched, trying to get more oxygen to her brain in an effort to stay awake. It did no good. Before Joe turned around, she felt her lids droop, and she didn't have the strength or force of will to open them.

"I can't believe the crowd," Joyce said as she helped serve cupcakes to the throng that filled the bakery.

"Catching a murderer is certainly giving us a boost in popularity," Angie said. She was busing the booths in the bakery that were full to bursting.

"I'll say," Tate agreed. "You can't pay for this kind of publicity."

"Hey, gorgeous." Roach appeared and looped an arm around Angie's shoulders. "Got a minute?"

Angie glanced at Mel, who nodded. They wound their way through the tables towards the door. Mel turned to find Tate watching them. He looked as if he were waiting for an earthquake to hit.

"You never told her how you feel," Mel said.

"I . . . It didn't seem fair," he said. "She's cared for me for so long. I was such an idiot. He makes her happy. How can I ruin that for her?"

"Are you kidding me?" Mel asked. "Well, it's nice to see your stupid streak will remain unbroken."

"What's that supposed to mean?" he asked.

"It means . . . Oh, forget it. If you're not man enough to tell her how you feel, then you don't deserve her," Mel said. "And if she moves to Los Angeles with him, then I am holding you personally responsible."

Tate opened his mouth to argue, but Mel

waved him off. She was not in the mood to hear it.

"The natives are getting restless, dear," Joyce said. "You'd better get on with the drawing."

Mel glanced around the room. It was true. These people had buttercream coursing through their veins. They were amped up and ready for the contest.

Mel stepped up onto a nearby stool. "Thank you, everyone, for coming to our bakery today and for entering our Fairy Tale Cupcake contest. Without further ado, I am going to draw the name of our lucky winner."

Tate hefted the box off the counter and held it up high for Mel.

"And the winner is . . . Wait." She paused. "Drum roll please."

Angie and Roach moved up closer to the front, and the two of them and Tate began to make rolling noises with their tongues.

"The winner is . . ." Mel said it again as she shoved her hand into the box full of slips and grabbed one from the middle bottom. She knew she couldn't play favorites, but she really wanted Marty to win. He and Beatriz were standing front and center, and even though he had a few years on her, they made a lovely couple.

She held the paper in her hands and then carefully unfolded it. "The winner is Olivia Puckett. *What?*"

Mel was so surprised, she stumbled from her stool and would have fallen if Tate hadn't caught her at the last second.

A delighted laugh that sounded more like a cackle erupted from the back of the bakery, and Mel glanced up to see Olivia standing there looking quite pleased with herself.

"You owe me a night on the town, Cooper," she said. "Tell your driver to pick me up at my house at seven."

With that, Olivia swept from the bakery. The crowd followed her until it was just Tate, Angie, Roach, Joyce, Mel, Beatriz, and a crestfallen Marty.

"How did she . . . ?" Mel muttered. "What are the odds?"

Mel glanced at the box. Had Olivia sabotaged her contest? Mel shoved her hand back into the box and pulled out a fistful of entries.

"Mel, you can't pick someone else," Angie said. "Olivia won it fair and square."

"Really?" Mel asked. She began to unfold the papers.

Olivia Puckett. Olivia Puckett. Olivia Puckett. "She got me. That evil, conniving, miserable woman got me."

"But how?" Angie began unfolding papers, too. Every one read the same name: *Olivia Puckett.*

Mel glanced up at her new friend. "I am so sorry, Marty. I don't know how she managed this."

"That's all right," he said. He turned to Beatriz. "I guess we'll have to cancel our date."

"What?" she asked. She tossed her dark hair over her shoulder and gave him an outraged look. "Are you ditching me?"

"I mean, I just figured you wouldn't want to go out with me if it wasn't a five-star restaurant and a limo."

"Martin Zelaznik, what kind of girl do you think I am?" she asked. "I said yes to you, not to a fancy restaurant. Now you pick me up at six, or don't ever bother showing up to another one of my yoga classes."

She strode towards the door, and Marty turned and grinned at Mel. He yanked the lapels of his suit jacket into place and hurried after her.

"All's well that ends well," Joyce said. "Well, if you don't need me anymore, I am going shopping. I still need to replace my heart attack dress."

"Maybe you could downgrade it to an

angina dress," Mel said.

"Funny, very funny," Joyce said. She blew them all an air kiss and left.

"Walk me out?" Roach asked Angie.

"Sure," she said.

Mel and Tate were silent as the door shut behind them.

" 'Louis, I think this is the beginning of a beautiful friendship,' " Mel said.

"Again with *Casablanca*?" Tate asked.

"It just seemed appropriate," Mel said.

Tate pulled his apron over his head. "I think 'We'll always have Paris' may be more accurate."

They were silent for a minute. Mel wanted to comfort her friend, but she didn't know how.

"Has she told you her decision?" he asked.

"No. You?"

"No."

"Maybe she doesn't know yet," Mel said.

Tate glanced through the front window, where Angie was wrapped in Roach's arms. "Maybe. Listen, I'm going to go."

He gestured to the back door, and Mel nodded. She understood. He was going to slip out the back so as not to have to see Angie and Roach up close. Understandable. She set about cleaning up the slips that littered the counter.

Olivia had gotten her good. She wasn't sure how, and she wasn't sure when, but she did know there would be payback involved.

It was hard to believe that a mere few weeks ago her mother had been in here giddily announcing her first date. And now, one of Mel's students sat in jail under arrest for the murder of Baxter Malloy. Rumor had it Poppy Gatwick had fled the state to be with her parents on Long Island. It appeared Jay had been right: Without the ability to buy Poppy pretty things, he couldn't buy Poppy. The perfect couple was not so perfect after all.

A pair of arms wrapped around her from behind, and Mel happily leaned against the familiar chest of Joe DeLaura.

"The jury convicted," he said.

Mel spun around in his arms with a joyous cry and hugged him tight. "You won, Joe, you won! That's wonderful. Let's go celebrate."

"No." He shook his head at her. Mel studied his face, and in his warm brown eyes she saw the same look that she had seen when she first realized she was in love with him.

"No?" she asked. "Don't tell me there's another case."

He grinned. "No, no case."

"Then what is it? You should be ecstatic, you should go out and pound some bubbly and howl at the moon."

"I had bubbly last night," he said. "While I watched you sleep."

Mel hung her head. "I fell asleep on you. I'm sorry. I tried so hard to stay awake, really, I did."

Joe pulled her close. "Don't be sorry. It made me realize what a selfish jerk I've been, falling asleep on you like I have. My only defense is that I just wanted to be with you, even if it was only in my sleep."

"Oh, Joe." She had thought she couldn't love him more than she already did. She was seriously mistaken.

"Holding you while you slept was one of the nicest evenings I've ever spent," he said. "I felt like everything was right in my world because I had you in my arms."

"I felt the same way about you all those nights I spent watching you sleep," Mel said. "If it was the only way I could have you, then that was fine with me."

He cupped her face and said, "Let's run away together."

Mel looked back out the window. Angie was here — for now. It was her turn to run the bakery for a while. Mel dropped her apron on the counter, took Joe's hand, and didn't look back.

RECIPES

KISS ME CUPCAKES
A mint chocolate chip cupcake with red and white swirled mint icing and a big Hershey's Kiss planted in the middle.

1 3/4 cups all-purpose flour
2 1/4 teaspoons baking powder
1/8 teaspoon salt
1 stick butter, softened
1 cup sugar
2 eggs, room temperature
1 teaspoon mint extract
1/2 cup milk
1 cup semi-sweet chocolate chips
1 bag Hershey's Kisses

Preheat oven to 350 degrees. Sift together the flour, baking powder, and salt. Set aside. In a large bowl, cream together the butter and sugar until light and fluffy. Add the eggs one at a time, beating well with each addition, then stir in the mint extract. Add the flour mixture alternately with the milk; beat well. Add the chocolate chips, after dusting with flour to keep them from sinking while baking. Bake for 15 to 17 minutes. Makes 18 cupcakes.

Mint Buttercream Frosting

1 cup (2 sticks) butter or margarine, softened
1 teaspoon mint extract
4 cups sifted confectioners' sugar
2–3 tablespoons milk
Red food coloring

In a large bowl, cream butter and mint extract. Gradually add sugar, one cup at a time, beating well on medium speed. Scrape sides of bowl often. Add milk and beat at medium speed until light and fluffy. Divide the frosting in half and put one half in a separate bowl. Use red food coloring to dye one half of the frosting red* and leave the other half of the batch white. To decorate the tops of the cupcakes, use a pastry bag with a star tip and work from the center of the cupcake to the edge, letting the stripe get wider (using more pressure on the bag) as it gets to the edge. Alternate the colors so that the frosting resembles a hard peppermint candy. Top with a Hershey's Kiss wrapped in silver foil.

Tip: When trying to make a deep red, start with a bright pink dye first and you won't have to use so much red to achieve the depth of color that you want.

ORANGE DREAMSICLE CUPCAKES
An orange cupcake topped with vanilla buttercream and garnished with a candied orange peel.

1 stick butter, softened
1 cup sugar
2 large eggs, separated and whites beaten until stiff
1 tablespoon orange zest
1 teaspoon orange extract
1 3/4 cups all-purpose flour
1/2 teaspoon salt
2 1/2 teaspoons baking powder
1/2 cup orange juice
Candied orange peels (for garnish)

Preheat oven to 350 degrees. Combine butter, sugar, egg yolks, zest, and orange extract in a large mixing bowl. Cream these ingredients together thoroughly. Sift flour, salt, and baking powder together in a separate mixing bowl. Add dry ingredients to creamed ingredients a third at a time alternately with the orange juice. Fold in the beaten egg whites. Spoon batter into cupcake liners until half full.

Bake for 15 minutes or until a toothpick inserted in the center comes out clean. Makes 18 cupcakes.

Vanilla Buttercream Frosting
1 cup (2 sticks) butter, softened
1 teaspoon clear vanilla extract
4 cups sifted confectioners' sugar
2–3 tablespoons milk (or whipping cream)

In a large bowl, cream butter and vanilla extract. Gradually add sugar, one cup at a time, beating well on medium speed. Scrape sides of bowl often. Add milk and beat at medium speed until light and fluffy. For best results, keep icing in refrigerator when not in use. This icing can be stored up to 2 weeks. Rewhip before using. Makes 3 cups of icing.

CUPID'S BLISS CUPCAKES
A white chocolate cupcake with a circle of white chocolate cream cheese icing around the edge with raspberries in the middle and drizzled with raspberry syrup on top.

1 1/2 cups all-purpose flour
1 teaspoon baking powder
1/2 teaspoon salt
1/3 cup butter, softened
3/4 cup sugar
2 large eggs, room temperature
4 ounces white chocolate, chopped
1 teaspoon vanilla extract
1 cup plus 1 tablespoon milk
Fresh raspberries

Preheat oven to 325 degrees. In a medium bowl, whisk together flour, baking powder, and salt. Set aside. In a small, microwave-safe bowl, melt the chopped white chocolate by heating it in 30-second intervals in the microwave. Stir well with a fork after each interval. The chocolate is ready when it's smooth when stirred.

In a large bowl, cream together butter and sugar. Beat in eggs one at a time, followed by the melted white chocolate and vanilla extract. Alternate adding the milk and the flour mixture. Divide batter evenly into prepared muffin cups.

Bake at 325 degrees for 20–23 minutes until a toothpick comes out clean or the tops spring back when lightly pressed with a fingertip. Makes 18 cupcakes.

White Chocolate Cream Cheese Frosting
4 ounces cream cheese, room temperature
1/4 cup butter, room temperature
1 ounce white chocolate, melted and slightly
   cooled
1 teaspoon vanilla extract
3 teaspoons milk or cream
2–3 cups confectioners' sugar

In a large mixing bowl, cream together cream cheese, butter, and melted white chocolate. Beat in vanilla extract and milk, then add in the confectioners' sugar gradually until the frosting reaches your desired consistency. It should be a bit stiff to allow piping along the edge of the cupcake. Transfer to a pastry bag fitted with a star tip and pipe a circle on the outer edge of each cupcake. Fill circle with fresh raspberries. Drizzle raspberry syrup (see below) on top.

Raspberry Syrup
7 cups raspberries, fresh or frozen (thaw
   slightly)
3/4 cup lemon juice
1 3/4 cups sugar
2 1/4 cups water
1 teaspoon vanilla extract

Combine raspberries, lemon juice, sugar,

and water in a saucepan and bring to a simmer over medium heat. Cook until raspberries are soft, about 15 minutes.

Strain raspberry mixture through a fine-mesh sieve; use the back of a spoon and press down to get all of the juice through the sieve. Discard raspberry seeds and pour extracted juices into pan. Simmer over medium-low heat until reduced by one-half or to the consistency of syrup, 20 to 25 minutes. Add vanilla extract at the end of cooking time.

Due to reader demand, I am including this cupcake recipe as mentioned in my last book, Sprinkle with Murder. *This is one of my faves and the cupcake that Mel makes when she has trouble sleeping — thus the name.*

MOONLIGHT MADNESS CUPCAKES
A chocolate cupcake with vanilla buttercream frosting rolled in shredded coconut and topped with an unwrapped Hershey's Kiss.

1 1/2 cups flour
3/4 cup unsweetened cocoa
1 1/2 cups sugar
1 1/2 teaspoons baking soda
3/4 teaspoon baking powder

3/4 teaspoon salt
2 eggs, room temperature
3/4 cup milk
3 tablespoons oil
1 teaspoon vanilla extract
3/4 cup water, warm
1 bag shredded coconut, sweetened
1 bag Hershey's Kisses

Preheat oven to 350 degrees. In a large bowl, whisk together flour, cocoa, sugar, baking soda, baking powder, and salt.

Add eggs, milk, oil, vanilla extract, and water. Beat on medium speed with an electric mixer until smooth, scraping the sides of the bowl as needed. Scoop into paper-lined cupcake pans and bake for 20 minutes, until a toothpick inserted in the center comes out clean. Makes 18 cupcakes.

Vanilla Buttercream Frosting
1 cup (2 sticks) butter, softened
1 teaspoon clear vanilla extract
4 cups sifted confectioners' sugar
2–3 tablespoons milk (or whipping cream)

In a large bowl, cream butter and vanilla extract. Gradually add sugar, one cup at a time, beating well on medium speed. Scrape sides of bowl often. Add milk and beat at medium speed until light and fluffy. For best results, keep icing in refrigerator when not in use. This icing can be stored up to 2 weeks. Rewhip before using. Makes 3 cups of icing.

To finish the Moonlight Madness Cupcakes, spread a generous amount of the vanilla buttercream frosting on top of each cupcake with a rubber spatula, then roll the top of the cupcake in a bowl of shredded coconut before the frosting dries so the coconut will adhere to the frosting. Top with an unwrapped Hershey's Kiss.

ABOUT THE AUTHOR

Jenn McKinlay has baked and frosted cupcakes into the shapes of cats, mice, and outer space aliens, to name just a few. Writing a mystery series based on one of her favorite food groups (dessert) is as enjoyable as licking the beaters, and she can't wait to whip up the next one. She lives in Scottsdale, Arizona, with her family. Visit her website at www.jennmckinlay.com.

The employees of Thorndike Press hope you have enjoyed this Large Print book. All our Thorndike, Wheeler, and Kennebec Large Print titles are designed for easy reading, and all our books are made to last. Other Thorndike Press Large Print books are available at your library, through selected bookstores, or directly from us.

For information about titles, please call:
(800) 223-1244

or visit our Web site at:

gale.cengage.com/thorndike

To share your comments, please write:

Publisher
Thorndike Press
10 Water St., Suite 310
Waterville, ME 04901